The Billionaire Bentleys 2

Lock Down Publications and Ca$h
Presents
The Billionaire Bentleys
A Novel by *Von Diesel*

The Billionaire Bentleys

Lock Down Publications
P.O. Box 944
Stockbridge, Ga 30281
www.lockdownpublications.com

Lock Down Publications
Like our page on Facebook: Lock Down Publications @
www.facebook.com/lockdownpublications.ldp

Book interior design by: **Shawn Walker**
Edited by: **Shamika Smith**

Von Diesel

Stay Connected with Us!

Text **LOCKDOWN** to 22828 to stay up-to-date with new releases, sneak peaks, contests and more…
Thank you!

Submission Guideline.

Submit the first three chapters of your completed manuscript to ldpsubmissions@gmail.com, subject line: Your book's title. The manuscript must be in a .doc file and sent as an attachment. Document should be in Times New Roman, double spaced and in size 12 font. Also, provide your synopsis and full contact information. If sending multiple submissions, they must each be in a separate email.

Have a story but no way to send it electronically? You can still submit to LDP/Ca$h Presents. Send in the first three chapters, written or typed, of your completed manuscript to:

LDP: Submissions Dept
P.O. Box 944
Stockbridge, Ga 30281

DO NOT send original manuscript. Must be a duplicate.

Provide your synopsis and a cover letter containing your full contact information.

Thanks for considering LDP and Ca$h Presents.

Von Diesel

Chapter One

"Out!" Red Bentley screeched, his face turning puce with anger. "I want you out."

Lady J Bentley, who was sitting at her dressing-table, brushing her hair, paled and said nothing.

"Pack up your bony ass and go," Red snarled. "Get the fuck out of my house. I've had enough of you." It was Saturday morning and he'd marched into her bedroom full of piss and vinegar. She had no idea what had caused this sudden confrontation, she just knew it was upon her with no warning.

"Why are you acting like this?" she demanded, standing up and facing him. "We haven't had a fight. Nothing's different."

"Everything's different," he replied. "Last night was spent in the company of younger women, vital women, women who were able to make me hard again. It finally dawned on me that I've been wasting the years I have left with a dried-up old snob."

"You're disgusting," she said, turning away from him.

"I found the life force I've been missing for the last six years," he roared. "You can't stand sex. Every time I'm on top of you, you lie there like a wooden board giving me nothing."

"I've done everything you've ever asked me to," she said, making a supreme effort to remain calm.

"Yes," he sneered. "Even sucked my cock when I've had to beg."

"How dare you speak to me in such a fashion?"

"I'll speak to you how I want."

"You can't possibly mean what you're saying."

"Every goddamn word," he replied impatiently, cracking

his knuckles.

"And where do you expect me to go?" she asked coldly. "Let us not forget that I left my husband and gave up everything to look after you for the last six years."

"Look after me?" he roared. "You make me sound like a decrepit old invalid, and that's something Red Bentley will never be."

"I did not call you an invalid."

"Who gives a fuck what you said? You're boring. All you do is nag me about traveling abroad and spend my money at an alarming rate. It's enough. I want you out. In the future, I plan on enjoying my freedom."

"Do you now?" she said, a slow fury building within her. "Well, plan away because I am not going any-where."

"What?" he said, his leathery face twisted with anger.

"You heard me."

"Do you understand who I am?" he yelled. "Once I bring in my lawyers, they'll force you out immediately."

"Call them," she said, refusing to back down. "I have a right to be here. This is my home too."

"I advise you," Red said, his rheumy eyes glittering with malice, "do not get into a pissing match with me because I can assure you that no woman has ever gotten the better of Red Bentley."

She regarded him for a long, silent moment. It was prob-ably true, no woman ever had. He'd managed to kill off three wives, and the fourth was a broken-down drunk who lived a pathetic life. But she, Lady J Bentley, was different. She was made of stronger stuff, and she refused to be intimidated by this churlish old man. She was smarter than he thought. She knew plenty about Red Bentley, things he would never want anyone to know.

"When we have negotiated a suitable settlement, and only then, I will consider leaving," she said evenly. "You can deal directly with me, or you can speak to my lawyers. Whichever you prefer."

"A settlement." He cackled. "We'll see about that."

"Yes, we will," she answered calmly, refusing to betreated like one of his whores. "Tell me, Red," she added, "exactly what surprise do you have in store for your three sons on Monday? How else are you planning on ruining their lives?"

"Ruining their lives?" he bellowed. "Those boys would be nothing without me. Look at what they've achieved."

"Yes," she said succinctly, "and, might I add, without an ounce of help from you."

"Bitch!" he muttered. "You know nothing."

"I know how you forced those two banks to withdraw from Touch's project. I also know you've been in touch with Patrick Sumter in Las Vegas, insisting that he pressure Krush for the money he owes. Not very fatherly acts, are they, Red?"

"I'm teaching them a lesson," he growled.

"They are grown men, Red. Why do you keep punishing them? What have they done to deserve this kind of treatment?"

"Have you been spying on me?" he shouted, his craggy face darkening. "How do you know all this?"

"I don't spy, I protect. And I might remind you that you will never find anyone who'll protect you the way I do."

"Bullshit!"

"And I should also warn you that if you think I spend money, start seeing other women and you'll find out how much they spend. I have made your home a place of calm and beauty. I entertain when you request me to. I even putup with the call-girls you meet at your secret apartment on 59th Street, the apartment you think I don't know about. Well, I do know about your whores, Red. And I know plenty of other things that I'm sure you wouldn't want to become public knowledge."

"Last night I got more action from a bunch of strippers than I've had from you in six years," he growled. "So, you can get your blackmailing ass out of my house because I have no use for it anymore. Do you understand what I'm saying? I'm finished with you. Finished. Done."

"You really are a vile man," she said, controlling the icy fury that helped her to stay strong.

"Then get the fuck out," he screamed.

"Not until I'm ready, Red. And that you can depend on."

***

On the way over to Chilly's hotel, Krush received another call. This time it was from Damiun Likely, who should have been on his way to Europe, but apparently was not.

"I need to see you, Krush," said Damiun, not sounding like his usual in control self. "It's urgent."

"Where are you?"

"My apartment," Damiun said, and gave him the address.

"I'm on my way to a client now. Soon as I'm through, I'll make it over to you."

Christ! Who the hell invented cell phones? People could reach you wherever you were, it was ridiculous. First Chilly, now Damiun. All he needed was a call from Lola Sanchez and his day would be complete.

***

"Draygo is not good man," Sadiya said, in a highly agitated state as she paced around her living room, her high heels clicking on the marble floor.

"You're not telling me anything new," Touch said evenly.

"Draygo is dangerous. You do not understand how dangerous he is."

"Maybe not, Sadiya. But I do understand that he's your problem, not mine."

"No, Draygo is our problem," she said vehemently. "I was never married to this man. The so-called papers he showed you are forgeries."

"I'm relieved to hear that."

"He can do bad things to us, Touch. Very bad things."

"I doubt it."

"In California," she said thoughtfully, "they kill people who get in your way."

"What?"

"In California, Robert Blake doesn't like his wife, so the newspapers say he kills her, or perhaps arranges to have it done. Phil Spector doesn't like the girl who comes back to his house, so poof, maybe he shoots her. We should do this to Draygo."

Jesus Christ! It was the same scenario that had crossed his mind. Coming from Sadiya, it seemed surreal. "How can you even think of something like that?" he said harshly.

"You want your daughter to be called illegitimate in the newspapers?" Sadiya said. "Camryn. Our Camryn."

"That won't happen."

"If Draygo is not silenced, it will."

"Has he contacted you?" Touch demanded.

"No," she said, looking away from him.

Immediately, he knew she was lying. Sadiya had never been a convincing liar.

"You have seen him," he said accusingly. "You might as well tell me the truth, Sadiya, because it will come out eventually."

"Alright," she admitted. "He came to my door lastnight. There was nothing I could do."

"And you let him in?" Touch said, shocked that she would be that stupid.

"What was I supposed to do? He informed the desk clerk he was my brother."

"Christ! What did he want from you?"

"Money."

"And?"

"I told him that I would talk to you."

"He's already getting money from me." A long beat passed. "Sadiya, if you swear to me that you have no connection with him, that the papers he has are indeed forged, then I can arrange to have him arrested."

"No," she said quickly. "Think of the headlines—"

"What headlines? If he's a fraud, whatever they write doesn't matter. I'll sue their asses."

"But you see, I did know him once, a long time ago,"she said, once again refusing to make eye-contact. "Draygo was a business acquaintance of one of my cousins."

"Jesus Christ!" Touch exploded. "Why didn't you tell methis before? You're unbelievable."

"I'm sorry, Touch. I—"

"Were you married to him, Sadiya?" he interrupted. "You'd better tell me because we're not playing games here."

"Absolutely not."

"Why should I believe you?"

"Because I tell you truth," she said defiantly.

"I hope so."

Sadiya began pacing again. "We must get rid of him, Touch," she said. "If we don't, there will be trouble."

"What trouble?"

"I know people who can handle this situation for us. It will cost fifty thousand dollars."

"Are you insane?"

"In Russia, we learn how to deal with the enemy." Had he really been married to this woman at one time?

"I will find out where he's staying," Sadiya continued. "I have friends in Moscow. They'll know."

"Oh, I see. You can just call Moscow and say, 'where is Draygo Kashif staying?' and they'll tell you. It's that easy?"

"I have connections," she said, in a low voice. "Get me the money and our problem will vanish."

"I refuse to pay to have someone killed," he said angrily. "This conversation is over."

"No, Touch, it's not. You must think about it overnight. We'll talk tomorrow."

"I can't tomorrow. It's my rehearsal dinner with Shemika."

"In the morning when your mind is clear."

"Didn't you hear me?" he said, exasperated. "I just told you that I'm busy tomorrow."

"You bring me cash," Sadiya said, not listening to a word he uttered, "and I will take care of everything. There is no need for you to be involved."

"No, Sadiya. Listen to me. No!"

"Touch, I understand men like Draygo. This is theonly way."

"We'll see about that."

***

Two clients, both demanding to see him, both claiming it was urgent. Ladies first, so Krush hurried over to Chilly's hotel.

He was let into her suite by the cousin who doubled as her useless assistant. Clad in baggy dungarees and a skimpy T-shirt emblazoned with the words C. Rose ROCKS, this cousin was a less attractive version of Chilly with stringy hair and a blank expression.

"Where is she?" Krush asked, striding into the suite, and looking around. "She told me it was urgent."

"In the bedroom," Chilly's cousin said, chewing gum. "You can go on through."

The bedroom was in darkness, drapes firmly closed. "Can somebody put a light on?" Krush said, groping his way into the room. "I can't see a thing."

Chilly flicked on the bedside light. She was propped in the middle of the bed, surrounded by the tabloids, several entertainment magazines, and a slew of discarded wrappers.

Krush immediately saw why she was so anxious to remain in the dark. The pretty young singer was featuring a lethal black eye and a badly swollen split lip.

"Who did this to you?" He demanded a redundant question because he already knew the answer.

"He didn't mean it," Chilly mumbled, in a little girl voice. "We were, like, fighting, and he kinda hit me by accident."

"Some accident," Krush said, scratching his head.

"I told you," she said, distressed that Krush didn't believe her, "it was a mistake. Brewsky wouldn't hit me on purpose."

"We should call the police," Krush decided.

"No!" Chilly shrieked, sitting up straight. "If I'd wanted

to call the cops, I would've done it last night. Brewsky was, like, upset because of the whole prenup thing. I should've given him what he wanted; I know I should."

"Chilly, do you still want me to be your lawyer?" Krush asked sternly. "Because if you do, you'd better start listening to me."

"I did listen to you," she answered sulkily. "Look where it got me."

"Where's Brewsky now?"

"He was here earlier, all kinda sorry," reaching for a tissue, "But I'm, like, so not speaking to him."

"I take it the marriage is off?"

"No way!" Chilly exclaimed, shocked at the thought. "I'm punishing him because I'm, like, mad he messed up my face. We're still getting married, though."

"Chilly," Krush said, as patiently as he could, because getting through to his youngest client when she imagined herself in love was not the easiest of tasks, "you can't be in love with a man who beats you up."

"It was a one-time thing, Krush," she explained, rubbing the tip of her nose. "He made me, like, a solemn promise that he'd never do it again."

"You'd better tell me how it happened," Krush said, resigning himself to the fact that Brewsky was going nowhere fast.

"Well," Chilly said tremulously, "we were, like, coming out of Ralph and Kacoo's' last night, and there were paparazzi everywhere. They were, like, pushing and shoving, trying to goad us into stuff. This made Brewsky even madder 'cause we'd already been fighting in the club."

"Where were your bodyguards?"

"My fault, 'cause we kinda ran out without them," she admitted sheepishly.

15

"Smart move."

"Sorry," she said, her voice getting smaller and smaller.

"And then?"

"Brewsky was like kicking one of the photographers out the way, so I tried to stop him. That's when he turned around and like accidentally punched me."

"Great!" Krush said, considering the ramifications.

"It's possible they might have, you know, got some of it on camera," Chilly admitted.

"Got some of what?" Krush asked, frowning. "Not Brewsky beating you up in public, I hope?"

"I suppose so," she said, shamefaced.

"Then I guess I should prepare for a lawsuit from the photographer?"

"He didn't get hurt," she whined. "Only me."

"Even better."

"I was wondering, Krush, if there's anything you can do to keep it out of the rags."

"Too late now, you should've called me last night. The photographers have already sold their shots."

"Can't we release a statement saying that, you know, it was all, like, an accident?"

"Let's see what they've got first. Then we'll talk about statements." He took a beat. "Have you seen a doctor?"

"Room Service sent up a raw steak last night," she said, pulling a disgusted face. "I put it on my eye. It stank up the whole room."

"How about your lip? Does that need attention?"

"Hurts," she said, in her little-girl voice.

"We should get you a doctor. You might need stitches." "Don't wanna see a doctor," she mumbled, holding back tears.

"I'm sure the hotel doctor is very discreet. I'll call the

concierge and see what he can arrange."

"Sorry, Krush," she said, even more tearful now. "I didn't mean for this to happen."

"It happened, Chilly," he said. "And you should think very seriously about marrying a man who treats you this way."

"I'm still marrying him," she said defiantly. "So you go ahead and arrange the wedding in Vegas. I told Brewsky that you'd give him the money from whoever buys exclusive rights to our wedding photos."

"And that didn't please him?"

"He was pissed when I said I couldn't do the million-dollars-a-year thing if our marriage didn't last."

"I think I should talk to him, straighten out a few things."

"No," she said quickly. "He'll just get mad at you and take it out on me. That's his way of dealing."

"Nice guy."

"He is, really he is," Chilly said, as if she believed it. "You've just gotta know him the way I do."

Women and abusive men, they never learned. Krush wished he could make her see the error of her ways, but Chilly was in love or lust, so right now she was seeing nothing.

He made a call, and soon after that a doctor arrived. Krush showed the portly man into the bedroom, then paced around the living room waiting for him to leave so he could get over to Damiun and sort out his drama, whatever it might be.

As the doctor emerged ready for a conversation, Krush's cell rang. He checked the caller ID, saw it was Chandra, and decided she could wait.

Once he'd finished conferring with the doctor and made sure Chilly was alright, he took off to see Damiun. On the way he called Chandra back. "What's up?" he asked brusquely.

"I'm in the middle of meetings. "I'm calling as a friend," Chandra said.

Hmm...sounded ominous. Maybe she was breaking up with him. Not such a bad deal, it would save him the trouble.

"That's nice, Chandra," he said, stifling a yawn. "I'm thrilled to hear it."

"I'm sorry, but I have bad news."

"More bad news?"

"There's been a mudslide," she continued. "Your house is more or less wrecked."

"My house?" he said, alarmed. "What are you talking about?"

"I was driving by to make sure everything was okay because of the rain, and it must have just happened. There were fire trucks and paramedics, everyone was wondering if there was anyone inside. I told them no."

"My house?" he repeated. "This is fucking impossible!"

"It's not my fault, Krush," she said, in an annoyingly

sanctimonious tone. "Blame it on the weather. It's still raining here."

"Jesus Christ!" he exploded. "How bad is it?"

"It's bad, Krush. Your house is virtually buried under a complete landslide of mud. We're lucky we weren't in it. We could've been buried alive."

"My house is buried with everything in it?" he said incredulously. "My house?"

"I'm afraid so."

"Call both my assistants. Get them over there immediately."

"I would, Krush, but I don't have their home numbers.

It's best if you do it."

"You really are a big help, aren't you?"

"If we lived together, I could be."

He clicked off his phone, contacted his main L.A. assistant, telling him to get over to his house and see what he could salvage. "There's a safe in there somewhere," he said. "Find it! And when you do, don't let it out of your sight."

Von Diesel

Chapter Two

"Come with me," Chanel said, beckoning Velvet to follow her. "I got a few minutes, so I'll take care of your eyebrows."

"I'm not sure if I—" Velvet began, scared that Chanel was going to ruin her. She liked her thick eyebrows, they gave her face character.

"You need it, sister," Chanel interrupted. "And I'm doing it for free, so let's go."

"Okay," Velvet said, getting up. Why not? She had nothing to lose except her eyebrows. Besides, Tristin Juzang had taken off an hour ago, so there would be no more brief encounters.

They went to the make-up room where Chanel sat her down in a chair, threw a towel round her shoulders and said, "Bet you've been told this many times, but I'm addingmyself to the list. Your face is incredible, major bone structure. Ever considered modeling?"

"Not really," Velvet replied. Staring at herself in the long row of mirrors.

"Modeling doesn't interest me."

"Do you realize that with a face like yours you could be making a shit-load of money modeling?"

"I could?"

"You bet, babe," Chanel said, taking a step back to study Velvet's face. "Want me to set you up with an agent?"

Could this day get any better? First Tristin, now this offer.

Things were definitely looking up. "Why are you being sonice?" she couldn't help asking.

"Because I've been there, done the whole waitressing gig," Chanel explained. "Oh, yeah, and I know all about people treating you as if you don't exist."

"You've got that right," Velvet said, thinking of the woman in the knockoff Armani.

"The reason I got into make-up was because somebody helped me," Chanel explained. "So…whenever I can, I try to give back."

"But you're so beautiful," Velvet said. "How come you're not a model?"

"I like what I do. It suits me," Chanel said, shrugging. "Besides, I'm too old to be a model now. I'm gonna be thirty soon."

"That's old?"

"In the modeling world it is," Chanel said, nodding to herself. "They call them dinosaurs."

"Who's a dinosaur?"

"Oh, Tyra Banks, Iman," Chanel said casually. "Any girl over the big three-O."

"Wow!"

"So, whaddaya think? Wanna give it a shot? Make yourself some real money. It worked for Whitney Houston. She was a successful model until she got into singing."

"Maybe I'll take you up on it," Velvet said tentatively.

"You should," Chanel said, producing a lethal pair of tweezers. "Now, don't go getting all panicky on me, 'cause I'm going way drastic on the eyebrow thing."

"You are?" Velvet said, wondering if it was too late to chicken out.

"Lean your head back and relax," Chanel said, encouragingly.

"Is this going to be painful?"

"Maybe," Chanel said, starting to pluck.

"Ouch!" Velvet yelled, almost leaping out of the chair. "That hurt."

"Course it hurts," Chanel said matter-of-factly. "Gottasuffer for beauty.

"I can tell. You got a forest growing there, girl."

"Oh, great!"

"I could wax 'em, less painful, but I don't have my equipment with me."

"I can put up with the pain," Velvet said, gritting herteeth. "As long as it'll look good."

"Suffer, hon. Believe me, it's a lot more fun than aBrazilian!"

"What's a Brazilian?"

"Man!" Chanel said, her hands moving swiftly. "You reallyare green."

Velvet closed her eyes and thought about the end result. Malshonda was always perusing the fashionmagazines and pointing out before photos of people like Madonna and Jennifer Lopez. they'd both featured extremely thick eyebrows: now they looked sensational. Maybe their raging success was all to do with their eyebrows.

Yeah, right!

"How do you think the shoot's going?" she asked, attempting to take her mind off the little stabs of agony as Chanel plucked away.

"It's rolling. You gotta love that raunchy beat."

"Do you know Slick Jimmy?"

"I know 'em all," Chanel replied. "We hang at the same clubs."

"That must be fun."

"Yeah, Jimmy is a cool dude. This is his big break, that is if he doesn't blow it."

"I'm into his music, not his lyrics," Velvet said, getting used to the pain. "I told Tristin Juzang that."

Chanel stopped what she was doing. "You told Tristin

you didn't like the lyrics?" she said, raising an eyebrow.

"Why?" Velvet asked innocently. "Isn't that okay?"

Chanel laughed as if she didn't quite believe what she was hearing.

"Nobody tells Tristin anything. That man is king."

"Well," Velvet said casually, "he asked my opinion, so I gave it."

"He did, huh?"

"I told him that I liked the beat, and that the lyrics were way too sexist. And so is the video, with all those girls sticking their boobs and butts in the camera. What kind of a message isthat sending out?"

"It's what the industry wants," Chanel pointed out. "Those in-your-face, sexy kinda videos sell mucho records."

"Too bad."

Chanel resumed plucking. "What's your deal, music wise?"

"I'm a singer-songwriter, more like, you know—"

"Who? Jill Scott?"

"No, she's jazz, and anyways, I hate comparisons. My mom was a singer," she added wistfully, remembering the times Fatima was actually singing. "Growing up, we always had music around. I was totally crazy about Sade."

"Ah…*Smooth Operator*. Now we have a classic," Chanel said. "Is that your kind of sound?"

"Yes and no. I hope I'm an original. I told Tristin, I can call him Tristin, can't I?"

"Dunno," Chanel said, with an amused expression. "Can you?"

"I don't see why not."

"Exactly how long were you talking with him?"

"Long enough that he gave me his card and suggested I bring him my demo."

"You'd better watch out," Chanel warned. "They all wantone thing, and us girls know exactly what that is. Tristin might be king, but underneath the bling, he is no different from all the other horn-dogs out there."

"I know that," Velvet said. "He's married, right?"

"Only about as married as a dude can get. And his old lady in the biz we call her Spenderella, you do not want to mess with that woman. No way."

"I'm not planning on doing so."

"Toshi's a piranha," Chanel warned. "If she catches you with her man, she'll beat your ass raw with her eight-hundred-dollar Manolos! And, hon, I am not kidding."

***

As soon as Malshonda got a break, she grabbed Velvetby the arm and hurried her over to the Craft Service table.

"I'm starving," Malshonda complained, grabbing a handful of potato chips and a can of Coke. "All this damn dancing is sapping my God given energy."

"You're doing great," Velvet said encouragingly. "You look better than any of them. You're the sexiest one out there."

"How big does my butt look?" Malshonda demanded, stuffing potato chips in her mouth. "Too big or just right?"

"I'm telling you, it's hot. The guys on the set are drooling big-time."

"I bet they are," Malshonda said, reaching for a sticky Danish. "Girl, what happened to you?" she suddenly exclaimed. "You're looking way different."

"Chanel plucked my eyebrows. You like?"

"Damn! Big improvement," Malshonda said, biting into the Danish. "Do you think she'd do mine?"

"Forget about my eyebrows, I have big news," Velvet

said, and proceeded to tell Malshonda about her encounter with Tristin.

"Oh…my…God!" Malshonda exclaimed, mouth dropping open, sugar decorating her chin. "I knew this was gonna be a righteous day!"

"Yes," Velvet said dreamily. "He didn't have his shades on and, Malshonda, he has these great eyes. Kind of penetrating and sexy."

"Huh?"

"You heard."

"Oh, man!" Malshonda said, taking another bite of Danish. "I don't dig the way you're sounding. Face it, girl, the dude is married, and you know we got a rule. Married men are a no-go zone."

"I'm not thinking of him in that way. I'm just saying he has very soulful eyes. They kind of look right through you. You know what I mean…intense."

"Sheeit!" Malshonda groaned. "You're falling in love."

"No, I'm not," Velvet protested.

"Hmm…" Malshonda said, taking a swig of Coke. "Wait 'til Kev finds out you met Mr. Big."

"I'm not telling Kev."

"How come?"

"Because I'll take Tristin my demo, see if anything works out and if it does—"

"Oh, it's Tristin now, is it?" Malshonda teased. "Whatever happened to Mr. Juzang."

"Don't screw with me, Malshonda. This is serious stuff."

"Poor Kev." Malshonda sighed.

"Why poor Kev?"

"Because you got it bad and that ain't good," Malshonda sang.

"Tristin Juzang is business," Velvet said earnestly. "He can help me."

"Oh, sure he can, with his big soulful eyes and his big soulful dick."

"You are such a bitch. It's not like that."

"It's always been like that, little cous'. From the first day you set your baby greens on him, you were wham-bam hooked."

"That's only because I admire his talent. He's special—"

"They're all special when they're standing there with a hard-on."

"Get off it, Malshonda."

"I will if you will."

In the afternoon, Vanessa, the current hot girl in several hit videos, including one with Usher, which she made sure everyone knew about as she arrived on set.

Vanessa was Puerto Rican, a sexy dark temptress with waist-length hair, a curvy body and major attitude. She thought she was a star and acted appropriately. Her job was to slink all over Slick Jimmy, while the so-called fat girls, in various stages of undress, undulated around him.

"That hoe is a bitch on wheels," Chanel confided. "I won't touch her. She travels with her own make-up crew, let them have the pleasure."

Clad in a scarlet slash of a dress, Vanessa was all over Slick Jimmy, who put up no objections.

After a couple of takes, Vanessa really started playing the diva. Stepping forward to confront Wahlee, she began to spew a litany of complaints in a harsh Brooklyn accent. "Dude, I ain't down with the way things are going here. I hate how you shooting me, the muthafuckin' lighting is shit. We gotta start again."

Malaki was not pleased. He stood for her many complaints for a while. When Slick Jimmy started getting into it, he blew a gasket. He informed Vanessa that if she didn't like it, she could walk.

She walked.

Malaki immediately called a break, went off in a corner and got on the phone.

A few minutes later, he came straight over to Velvet. "You were the girl talking to Tristin earlier, right?" She nodded. "Velvet, that's your name?" She nodded again. "Okay, Velvet, it seems you got yourself a gig."

"Excuse me?"

"Tristin wants you in the video."

"Me?"

"Yes, you."

"Doing what?" she asked blankly.

"Replacing Vanessa."

"I'm a singer, not a dancer."

"You're calling Vanessa a dancer?" he said, with an amused expression. "I don't think so."

"But—"

"Listen to me," he said impatiently, "all you gotta do is the same as her, drape yourself around Slick Jimmy and look smoking hot. You can do that, huh?"

"In case you haven't noticed, I've got a sprained ankle and a burned arm."

"We'll cover your arm, and no moving, just draping."

"Look, I—"

"Chanel, Fantasia," Malaki yelled, cutting her off. "Get over here. Tristin wants this girl to look hot. She needs make-up, hair extensions, the works. Fantasia, see if she'll fit into Vanessa's dress, and I wanna see some kinda fur wrap covering her arm. Work it, ladies, we're way behind."

Velvet shook her head. Now her day was totally surreal.

What exactly had she done right?

And yet, why not? Hadn't she been wishing for a break?

Chanel whisked her back into the make-up room andsat her down in the chair again. "See what happens when you get your eyebrows plucked," she quipped. "Girl, I am gonna make you look fine."

"This is crazy," Velvet said, shaking her head. "How did it happen?"

"Tristin says jump, everyone jumps," Chanel replied, stepping back for a minute, and studying Velvet's face witha critical eye. "Guess you made some impression. Did they tell you how much they're paying you?"

"We didn't get into that. Should I ask for the same as Malshonda?"

"Forget it," Chanel said, beginning to apply a creamy make-up base to Velvet's face with a damp sponge. "Tell "em you want a thousand bucks 'cause you're a feature player."

"A thousand?" Velvet gasped. "They'll never pay that! It'sa fortune."

"You want me to tell 'em?" Chanel said, working away. "I'm tight with those guys."

"Could you do that?"

"Sure, and when you're a big singing star, you can hire me as your personal make-up artist. Oh, and if anyone asks, you're a member of the union."

"Is that okay to say?"

"Man," Chanel said, shaking her head, "Somebody's gotta teach you how to deal. How old are you?"

"Nineteen. I can deal. I've been around."

"Nineteen, huh? You're still a baby. and big bad Tristin's shining his light on you, so watch out because you gotta be real careful."

"Of what?"

"I told you once, I'll tell you again. Tristin is a major player," Chanel said, applying pale copper eye shadow to Velvet's eyelids with her finger.

"A big, fat, major player."

"As long as he likes my demo."

"And if he does, what you gonna do?" Chanel asked, standing back to survey her work. "You gonna fuck him and hope that lands you a recording contract? 'Because if That's your game, you'd better remember to make him wait until after you sign a contract."

Velvet shrugged. "I have no plans in that direction."

"Maybe you don't, but you can bet your ass Tristin does."

"Like you said, he's married."

"In the hip-hop world being married means nothing," Chanel announced, producing a soft beige lip gloss.

"Those guys are like athletes, screwing around is their national pastime. Man," she added, rolling her eyes, "I could tell you stories."

"You sound so jaded." Velvet sighed. "I'm sure they're not all like that."

"Sure, babe, believe what you like, but I'm giving you the real truth."

"If that's the truth, then it's sad."

"Allow me to tell you what those guys do," Chanel said. "They nail a beautiful girl, use her for as long as it amuses them, then the fuckers move on. Oh, yeah, and if the wife finds out, they zip down to the jewelry store and buy wifey-pie another ten-carat Bentley ring. What the fuck? it's only money."

"Why are you telling me this?"

"Because you're new, and you're a genuine beauty, especially now I've dealt with your damn eyebrows!"

"Oh, thanks, this is all happening because of my eyebrows, right?"

"Listen to me and learn. Tristin always goes for the beauties. Like Prince, his bag is to score the prize. and right now, you're it."

"You know, Chanel, in spite of what you think, I have been around. Working as a waitress, you get to knowexactly what most guys want. Besides, I have a boyfriend.I promise you; I can look after myself."

"I'm sure you can, hon. The only things is, you're moving into a whole different league now. So, all I'm saying is, watch it."

"I will."

"Do not believe the hype and the promises, and make sure, whatever they promise, see your own lawyer and getit in writing."

"Thanks, That's good advice. I think."

"Free, too," Chanel said, applying a dark contouring blush to Velvet's cheekbones.

"Trouble is, I don't have a lawyer," Velvet said ruefully.

"Hmm…" Chanel responded, with the hint of a smile. "Now why am I so not surprised?"

Von Diesel

Chapter Three

When Famous arrived at the video shoot, Chanel was still busy working on Velvet's face. "Hang around if you want," Chanel said, stopping to give him a quick peck onthe cheek. "I'll be through soon."

"No," he said. "Rap is not my thing. I gotta get moving."

"At least say hello to Velvet while you're here."

"Who's Velvet?"

"The new girl on the block," Chanel said, winking atVelvet. "And she's sitting right here, babe."

"Hey," he said, giving Velvet a quick look through the mirror.

"Hey," Velvet responded, equally casual.

The fact that they barely exchanged glances surprised Chanel because she'd thought Famous would be all over the exotically beautiful girl. Hmm…perhaps he was in love.

"Did you call that number?" she asked, still working onVelvet's face.

"Tried it a few times, no answer," he said, cracking his knuckles. "Guess I'll have to wait until Monday."

Then it occurred to him that on Monday Kareema would be in New York.

"Man! Nothing was ever easy."

"You want a coffee, anything?" Chanel offered.

"No, thanks, Chanel. You're busy, so I'm taking off. I'll call you later."

He left the studio, and on the way to Eddie's apartment, he started to feel guilty that he hadn't contacted his mother. As soon as he got to Eddie's, he picked up the phone before he changed his mind. "Mom?" he said, when Sukari answered.

"Now that's a word I haven't heard in a long time," Sukari responded, sounding relatively sober. "It'sFamous," he said, immediately groping for a cigarette.

"I guessed it was since you're the only person who calls me Mom and you are my son. Not that I've heard from you in a long time," she added reproachfully.

"I've been living in Italy," he said, wishing she could sound a little happier to hear from him. "You knew that."

"Where are you now?"

"Back in New York. I, uh…flew in for a few days."

"What for?"

"To meet with Red," he said, knowing that piece of information would not go down well.

"That bastard," she said bitterly. "Why would you want to meet with him?"

"He kind of summoned me. Sent me a ticket."

"Oh," she said, pouncing. "He summons and you jump."

"Yeah, Mom," he admitted. "I guess I jumped. But he is my dad, and Lady J insisted it was important."

"You spoke to her? That phony witch."

"She's the one who called," he explained. "And when they arranged for the ticket, I thought I'd take advantage ofa free trip. You know, get to see you and all."

"No such thing as a free trip, Famous," Sukari said ominously. "You'll end up paying, one way or the other."

"Maybe," he said, inhaling poisonous smoke.

"Your father's never going to change," Sukari said flatly. "I know that. When do I get to see you?"

"Do you want to?" he replied, remembering that the last time he'd seen her they'd had a huge fight. He couldn't even remember what it had been about.

"You could drive out to the house tomorrow," she suggested. "I'm here. I never go anywhere."

"I dunno, Mom," he said. "I gotta meet someone at the airport, then I promised Touch that I'd drop by his rehearsal dinner tomorrow night."

"Touch?" she said. "Since when are you close to him?"

"He invited me, I thought I'd go."

"Why?"

"Hey," Famous said, getting off the subject of family, "any chance of you coming into the city?"

"For what?" she snapped. "I hate the city. I hate being any place where I'm forced to breathe the same air as Red Bentley."

"Then we should try to get together next week."

There was a long silence, finally broken by Sukari. "Have you seen him yet?" she asked.

"Who?" he said, playing dumb, although he knew exactly whom she meant.

"Who do you think?" she said, sounding peeved. "That son-of-a-bitch I was married to."

"Uh, yeah, I saw him," Famous replied, trying to keep it light. "He turned up at Touch's bachelor party."

"What is this family-reunion time?" she said, a familiar slur creeping into her voice. "All of a sudden it's Touch this and Touch that. I'm your family, not those half-brothers."

"I know, Mom."

"Is Krush there too?" she asked, taking off on a fact-finding mission.

"Yeah, he's around."

"I'm sure you're aware it was him who paid for you to goto Italy, get into rehab and straighten yourself out."

"Who did you hear that from?"

"I have my sources. You should thank him. I'm positive

Touch didn't put a hand in his pocket. Tight bastard," she added disdainfully. "Exactly like his father."

He heard the clinking of ice in a tumbler, another familiar sound from his childhood. Sukari had always started the day drink in hand, it was among his earliest memories. "You doing okay, Mom?" he asked, treading carefully. "You're not drinking, are you?"

"I had a glass of water," she said belligerently. "Is that alright with you, Mr. Reformed Alcoholic?"

To avoid a fight, he hurriedly dropped the subject. "So...are you with anybody now?" he asked, keeping it casual. "Some handsome young stud?"

"None of your damn business," she told him, her words definitely tripping. "And you'd better behave yourself around my gentleman friends because, if I recall correctly, last time you got the bejesus beaten out of you."

Oh, great. Fond memories. Stoned as he'd been, there was no forgetting the low life she'd been supporting at the time.

Big fucking deal, so he'd thrown a few insults the loser's way. How was he supposed to know the creep was a professional boxer?

"I'll call you tomorrow, Mom," he said, suddenly overcome with a desperate urge to get off the phone.

"Do that," she said sourly. "If you can find the time."

He put down the phone and stubbed out his cigarette. One thing for sure, she'd certainly managed to wipe the smile off his face. Unfortunately, there was nothing new about that.

***

Touch was seething. What kind of game was Sadiya playing, and how could he find out?

It was all too suspicious. First Draygo turned up at his office, then Sadiya claiming she was not married to the Russian, when she knew perfectly well he'd seen the marriage papers.

Were they forged? Should he call in an expert?

No, he couldn't do that because it meant bringing in people who would then know his business.

Goddamn it! He was trapped in an impossible situation.

He called Shemika. "You never made it to brunch," he said accusingly, ready to vent his bad mood on someone.

"I'm so sorry," she said apologetically. "It wasn't my fault. Grams was in one of her talkative moods and it was impossible to get away."

"How is Grams doing?" he asked, softening because none of this was Shemika's fault and he shouldn't be taking it out on her. The truth was that she and Camryn were the only two worthwhile people in his life.

"Brilliant for ninety," Shemika answered cheerfully. "Shelooks better than either of us."

He didn't laugh. He wasn't in the mood for laughing. "So tonight, we'll have that quiet dinner, just the two of us."

"I was hoping to get an early night," Shemika responded.

"I'll make sure you get home in time," he promised.

There was a long silence before Shemika broke it, asking, "Is everything okay, Touch?"

"I told you, I have a lot on my mind business-wise. We'll talk later."

"Very well," she said reluctantly because she still felt unbelievably guilty, and she wasn't looking forward to spending time alone with Touch.

"I'll pick you up at eight," he said, still thinking about Sadiya and the devious plan she was plotting. Fifty thousand to kill someone, and she was under the impression he'd come up with the money. Oh, no, he was much too smart for that.

***

By the time Krush reached Damiun's Likely's, apartment, he'd made a decision. He was going to hop a plane to L.A., stay a few hours and fly right back for the Monday morning meeting with Red. Not only was he worried about his house but there was the matter of his safe, currently stuffed with two hundred and fifty thousand dollars in cash ready to be transported to Vegas and Patrick Sumter. He could not afford to lose track of that money.

Damiun's New York apartment, once featured on the cover of Architectural Digest with an eight-page spread inside, was a salute to sleek modern style. Damiun was an avid student of architecture: he enjoyed clean lines, structural simplicity, and stark furniture.

A barefoot Damiun answered the door himself. Wearing rumpled chinos and a loose shirt, he looked worried. There was no sign of any entourage.

"What's up?" Krush asked, walking in.

"WhatsApp is extremely embarrassing," Damiun replied, leading Krush through to the pristine kitchen.

"Whenever I'm summoned to anyone's apartment it's always about something embarrassing," Krush replied, perching on a chrome stool. "Not to worry, Damiun, I've heard it all and then some."

"Can I fix you a health drink?" Damiun inquired, busying himself chopping mangoes, bananas, and papayas, then tossing them into a blender with some rice milk.

"Not really," Krush said. "I kind of indulged myself last night and now I'm suffering the consequences. I'll have coffee, that's if you're making it."

"Coffee's no good for you," Damiun said. "I refuse to keep it in the apartment."

"Then I repeat," Krush said, "what's up?"

Damiun switched on the blender and was silent for a long moment as the fruit tossed and turned. Then he switched it off, poured his drink into a tall glass and gave a long-drawn-out sigh. "Uh...I guess we all do things we prefer to keep quiet, especially when you're an actor in the public eye."

"What're you trying to tell me?"

"It's not that I'm ashamed," Damiun said hesitantly, "but I realize that if this got out it could ruin my career."

"Keep going," Krush encouraged.

"Well," Damiun said, gulping down his health drink, "there are times when I walk a dangerous street."

"And what street would that be?" Krush asked, although he already suspected what the movie star was about to reveal.

"Look, I'm not trying to hide anything from you, Krush," Damiun said, speaking fast. "But please, this is between you and me. Lawyer privileges, right?"

"Of course."

Damiun set his glass on the counter. "I'm gay," he said, in a barely audible voice.

"I gather there's a problem?"

"A big problem," Damiun said. "Last night, I met a man."

"Yes?" Krush said, anticipating what he was about to hear.

"He was nice-looking, clean-cut," Damiun continued. "Rough trade isn't my style. I invited him back here, and we, uh...had a good time—"

"Can I interrupt?" Krush asked, flexing his fingers.

"Go ahead."

"Where was your girlfriend?"

"We have an arrangement. She's, uh...kinda into women, career-wise it suits both of us. So far, we've managed to fool the media."

"This is getting more complicated by the minute," Krush commented.

Damiun pushed a hand through his thick hair. "I realize you're shocked," he said, his boy-next-door face serious.

"Who, me?" Krush replied. "I'm a liberal, Damiun. Whatever you do is your business. I couldn't care less."

"I always knew I liked you," Damiun said, relieved that he wasn't being judged.

"Fill me in on what happened next."

"Well, the guy and I had our fun. And, um, when he was leaving, I offered him money."

"Was he a professional?"

"No, he wasn't. And as soon as I tried to hand him the money, I realized I'd made a big mistake."

"How did he react?" Krush asked, mentally picturing the scene.

"He became extremely insulted and angry. 'Who the fuck do you think you are?' he began screaming at me. 'Big fucking movie star hiding in the closet. You think you can buy everything and everyone. Well, I've got a newsflash for you, you can't. I can blow your image apart in a heartbeat.'"

"What happened then?"

"He asked me if I knew what he did. I told him I had no idea."

"Give me the clincher."

"Turns out, he's a journalist for a prominent gay magazine. Believe me, I might've got fucked last night, but now I'm really fucked. What are we going to do, Krush? What the hell are we going to do?"

Von Diesel

Chapter Four

Why did crises always happen on weekends? Lady J Bentley was unable to reach her lawyer, who happened to be on a three-day fishing trip to the Bahamas. She needed to speak to him but, in the meantime, she decided it was best to carry on as if nothing had happened. It was not unusual for Red to experience fits of unreasonable rage, but this time his rage was directed at her, and she did not appreciate it. The fact that he'd demanded she'd 'get out' was shocking. Oh, yes, over the years they'd been together they'd had fights over inconsequential things, but never anything like this.

She soon realized it would be prudent to put her time to good use. Since their initial morning blow-out, she had not seen Red. According to his precious housekeeper, Fatima, and what kind of a name was that for a housekeeper? He had left the house saying he would not be back until late.

Lady J suspected he'd gone to his so-called secret apartment, the one he hadn't realized she knew about where he was probably entertaining the whores that he'd come into contact with at Touch's bachelor party.

She had a good mind to call Touch and confront him, but then she thought why do that? Touch wasn't responsible for his father's vile behavior.

Instead, she began a systematic search of Red's private office, going through his desk drawers, opening every file, checking out his emails, inspecting every letter and document. There was a copying machine in his assistant's room, and since his assistant was never there on weekends, she made a copy of anything she thought might be useful. At one point, Fatima entered the room and had the audacity to ask what she was doing.

"Excuse me?" Lady J said, giving the woman an imperious look. She'd always hated Red's housekeeper, the sleazy black woman who didn't even look like a housekeeper, more like a gone-to-seed showgirl. "Are you actually asking me what I'm doing in here?"

"You're at Mr. Bentley's private computer," Fatima pointed out, crossing her arms. "Mr. Bentley does notallow anyone to use it."

"Do you realize who you're talking to?" Lady J said, amazed at the woman's nerve.

"Yes, I realize, Lady Bentley," Fatima replied, holding her ground. "But Mr. Bentley has told me many times that nobody is to come in here."

"I am working under his instructions," Lady J said, furious at this interruption. "Therefore, I suggest you take it up with him if you have any problems. And if you dare to question me again, I will make sure you are fired."

Fatima gave her an insolent stare and left the room.

Lady J decided that if she remained in residence, she would definitely make sure Red got rid of the woman, although she'd tried in the past and had no luck.

Red Bentley liked to hang onto his servants. He actually imagined that by keeping people in his employ a long time it ensured their loyalty. Lady J knew it to be exactly the opposite.

***

As soon as Krush had finished with Damiun Likely, he took a cab to the airport, not bothering to check out of his hotel because he'd be back the next day.

On the way to Kennedy, he spoke to Chi-rone, his young African American assistant, who was usually very reliable. "I'm flying in," he said curtly. "On my way to the airport now."

"There's no point in you coming to L.A.," Chi-rone argued. "I'm sorry to be the one to tell you, but your house is a no-go area."

"What are you talking about?"

"The city has it red-tagged as a possible slide down the hill."

"Son-of-a-bitch!" Krush said tersely. "Did you find my safe?"

"They won't let anyone near the house."

"Chi-rone," he said, in a voice that meant he would accept no argument, "I want you to go back there, break in and get my goddamn safe. That's if you value your job."

"You don't understand what's going on here," Chi-rone said, attempting to explain. "It's non-stop torrential rain, huge storms, and people are being swept away. In Conchita, houses were buried under the mudslide. Many people lost their lives."

"C'mon," Krush said, refusing to believe it was as bad as Chi-rone was making out. "This is L.A. we're talking about."

"I know," Chi-rone said miserably, "and it's a disaster."

"I'm flying in anyway. Have a car and driver at the airport, and meet me at my house."

"You're not listening to me, Krush. There's no house to meet you at."

"Get in your fucking car, go to my fucking house and stay there," Krush said, losing it.

He managed to get a United flight out. Unfortunately, there were no seats left in first class, so he had to make do. He complained bitterly to anyone who cared to listen.

Jeez! he thought, I'm turning into my father's son. *Screaming at my assistant to break into a house that's been red tagged. Bitching about not being in first class. What happened to me?*

Then he remembered Damiun and his problem. It was a whole lot bigger than his. Damiun's entire career was at stake, and what was he going to do about that?

He'd told Damiun not to worry and that it was taken care of.

"I am worried," Damiun had replied, throwing him an I-trust-you-implicitly look. "Nobody knows about this except you, Krush. I'm depending on you." What was he supposed to do? Pay the guy off?

Yes, that was usually the answer. Damiun had said he would pay as much as he had to, anything to shut the journalist up.

Krush nodded. In his experience, most people could be bought. It all depended on the price.

***

Toying with her meal, Shemika couldn't help noticing that Touch definitely had something on his mind. This wasno big deal because she did too. Valiantly, she tried to make conversation, but Touch kept on staring off into space as if his thoughts were elsewhere. She hoped andprayed he hadn't found out about her one wild night.

The waiter cleared their dishes and asked if they wanted coffee and the dessert menu.

Shemika shook her head. Touch requested the check. "Are you sure you're ready for the rehearsal dinner tomorrow night?" Shemika asked, determined to get him talking before they left.

"I'm ready," he said curtly. "Why wouldn't I be?"

She sighed and picked up her glass of wine. "You saw Sadiya today, didn't you?"

He nodded. "How did you know?"

"She always puts you in a bad mood."

"You think so?"

"It's true, Touch. You're much happier when you deliverCamryn to her nanny, and you don't have to see your ex."

"Problem is, Sadiya's always there," he said, grimacing. "There's no avoiding her. She gets her kicks torturing me."

"Something else is bothering you," Shemika said, leaning across the table. "I wish you'd tell me what it is."

"Business problems," he answered gruffly. "Nothing I can't solve."

"It's helpful to share, Touch. After all, we are getting married soon."

"Yes, sweetheart, and I for one can't wait," he said, as the waiter brought the check. "You do know how much I love you, don't you?" he said, throwing down his black American Express card.

No, she didn't. It would be nice if he told her more often. And why had he so readily accepted her no-sex-before-marriage rule?

Then there was the biggest question of all, what had made her sleep with a total stranger? How could she ever explain? Abruptly, he stood up. Dinner was apparently over.

***

The plane ride to L.A. was non-stop bumpy all the way. By the time Krush arrived he realized he might have madea mistake. He'd told Chi-rone to have a car and driver at the airport. The car was waiting, and so was the rain: itwas still pouring down in windswept torrents. Chi-rone was right, L.A. was one big mess.

The driver insisted on telling him bad-weather stories all the way down the freeway.

Krush sat in the back wishing the goddamn driver would

shut the fuck up. He needed to concentrate on everything he had to take care of. First there was Damiun, a big priority. Then Chilly and her problems. His house, exactly how damaged was it? And of course, Patrick Sumter and the money he owed.

When he reached his home, he had to give Chi-rone credit because even though it was pitch black and late, the young man was sitting in his SUV waiting patiently for him. Now that was loyalty.

Krush got out of the car, ran over, and tapped on Chi-rone's window. "Did you get my safe out?" he yelled, over the pounding rain.

Chi-rone rolled down his window and handed him a flashlight. "Take a look, Krush," he shouted. "Your house is buried under a ton of mud. I can't get anywhere near the front door, can't even see it."

Krush took the flashlight and walked over. Things were far worse than he'd imagined. There was no house, just a giant mountain of mud, and large signs red tagging his property.

"What arrangements have you made about getting it cleaned up?" he yelled, thinking that once they got rid of the mud, his house would emerge pristine and undamaged.

Yeah, sure.

"Can't do anything until the rain stops," Chi-rone replied, trying to shelter them with an umbrella. "Then they'll be able to bring in heavy dredging equipment and get to work."

"Fuck!" Krush said, getting thoroughly wet, his shoes sinking into the soggy ground. "I came home to this."

"I did warn you," Chi-rone pointed out. Anxious to find out. "I'll deal with it, Krush. I'll do everything I can."

"Fuck!" Krush repeated, shaking his head as rain soaked

through his clothes. "This is a fucking joke."

After dinner, Touch took Shemika home, pecked her on the cheek and that was that. Another unsatisfying evening with a man she wasn't sure she still loved.

Upstairs in her apartment, she wandered from room to room, restless and confused. Was she doing the right thing? Could she go through with it? Was Touch the perfect man for her?

Oh, sure, it was easy for Megan to tell her he was, but Megan wasn't marrying him. She was, and she couldn't get her night with Eddie Rogers out of her head. His handsome face kept floating in front of her, his mesmerizing blue eyes, his muscular body, and the way he'd held her in his arms... She wondered if he was thinking about her.

Probably not. It was likely he was one of those guys who slept with lots of women, and never gave them a second thought. How sad was that?

And yet, even if it was true, she still couldn't stop thinking about him. And even worse, she didn't want to.

***

By the time Krush checked into the Four Seasons, it was past midnight. He'd instructed Chi-rone to book him out on an early-morning flight to New York, so after a good night's sleep he'd be on his way back.

After ordering a bowl of hot soup and a medium rare steak from room service, he picked up the phone and finally reached Patrick Sumter in Vegas.

"Where are you?" Patrick asked gruffly.

"Back in L.A." he said, not about to take any shit. "My house has been destroyed."

"Didn't do it," Patrick dead panned.

"That's not funny," Krush snapped.

"You get what you ask for," Patrick said, adding a casual, "How do you like your New York gift?"

"She was very accommodating," Krush replied, thinking how much he couldn't stand this man. "Especially when she took off with my gold Rolex. Was that part of the plan, or are you too cheap to pay her the going rate?"

Patrick laughed. It wasn't a friendly sound. "I'm expecting you here tomorrow with my money."

"Your money happens to be in my safe, and right now my safe is buried under a mudslide somewhere in my house. So, I'm afraid you'll have to wait."

"You shitting me?" Patrick growled.

"Send one of your goons to check my story. Go ahead, maybe they can dig it out."

"Does this mean you're not coming tomorrow?"

"No, Patrick," Krush said, clenching his jaw. "You'll get your goddamn money next week. Right now, I'm involved with more pressing problems, like nowhere to live, everything I own is destroyed, and I gotta fly back to New York for a meeting. As I said, you'll have to wait. And oh yeah, don't bother sending me any more visitors."

"Quit giving me orders, you dumb prick."

"You're the dumb prick," Krush answered, beyond caring. "I'm offering you a chance to host Chilly Rose's wedding at your hotel, which would mean millions of dollars' worth of free world-wide publicity, and you're not even entertaining the idea. If you were smart, you'd speak to your PR people and listen to what they have to say. I'm giving you twenty-four hours to get back to me. Then I'm calling Peter Morton at the Hard Rock. He's a smart guy, he'll get it. And don't worry, you'll get your fucking money!" He slammed the phone down. Man, it felt good!

Naturally, he couldn't sleep. How could he? His house was wrecked with everything he owned in it, and how could he stop himself thinking about all the things he'd lost? It was making him feel sick. His house was a symbol of everything he'd achieved. Now it was gone, and there was nothing he could do about it. Outside, the rain continued to pour down. Talk about losing control, it was not a pleasant feeling.

Von Diesel

Chapter Five

Acting as Velvet's spokesperson, Chanel went to Malaki, the director, and informed him that Velvet required a thousand dollars a day for the two days she'd be workingon the video.

"It's already set," Malaki said. "She's getting two thousand a day, Tristin's instructions. The dude is into her."

"We need it in writing," Chanel replied, trying not to look too surprised that this was all so easy.

"In writing? Or how about she gets paid cash?" Malaki suggested. "That way she puts it into her pocket and walks away."

"Cash will do nicely," Chanel said, thinking that she should have asked Velvet for commission. Not seriously, though, Chanel's latest philosophy was all about giving back, and it was working. She'd met Lenny D, and he was the first decent man she'd hooked up with in a long time.

When Chanel told Velvet about the money, there was a stunned silence. "Two thousand dollars a day?" Velvetsaid at last. "A day? Are you sure?"

"Don't sweat it. They were probably paying Vanessa plenty more. Besides," Chanel added, teasing her, "Tristin likes you. He really likes you."

"He does?" Velvet said, remaining cool.

"So says Mr. Director."

Velvet didn't even want to ask what that meant. She took off to find Malshonda, who was in a complaining mood. "Ha!" Malshonda bitched when she told her. "I gotta shimmy around with my ass hanging out, shoving itin the freaking camera, and all you gotta do is stand there glammed up like some kinda diva." Malshonda stared at her reflection in a full-length mirror. "Sheeit! This ain't fair."

"You'll think it's even less fair when you hear what

they're paying me," Velvet said excitedly.

"More than I'm getting?" Malshonda said, narrowing her eyes.

"Try two thousand a day," Velvet said, still in shock that she was about to make such an unbelievable amount of money for basically doing nothing.

"Man!" Malshonda yelled, jumping up and down. "We're freaking richer than freaking shit! We can get ourselves that flat screen TV we've been talking about forever. I ain't even minding that you're getting more than me."

"First, we pay our bills," Velvet said, thinking about what a relief that would be. "Do you know how many bills we've got piled up that I keep on juggling 'cause you refuse to deal with them?"

"That's because you're better at it than me," Malshonda said, adjusting her costume. "You're the smart cookie, I'm the booty queen!"

"That's right," Velvet agreed, laughing.

"You'd better call your mama," Malshonda said.

"Why would I do that?"

"Because you should tell her to drop by my mom's to-morrow night. We'll all celebrate together."

"I'm not sure I want to see her," Velvet said uncertainly. "I still don't get why she couldn't have told me about my dad before. It's not fair she waited all these years."

"She probably figured you wouldn't wanna know you had a dead daddy and that it was better for you to grow up with, you know, some kinda hope."

"Yeah," Velvet said bitterly, "false hope."

"Let's not get into it now," Malshonda said. "There's too much slamming shit going on."

"When am I supposed to get into it?" Velvet muttered,

almost to herself.

"What time's our call tomorrow?" Malshonda asked, quickly changing the subject.

"Ten. According to Chanel, they're not into starting early in the rap world."

"Man, Chanel is the coolest," Malshonda said enthusiastically. "She's gonna fix my eyebrows tomorrow. I'm telling you, for sure it's the eyebrows that got you the gig. Just you wait 'til Tristin sees you now. He's gonna dump his old lady and the two of you'll hook up permanently. Mrs. Tristin Juzang. Try that on for a tight fit. It's all good, girl."

"Zip it, Malshonda," Velvet said, looking around to make sure no one had heard. "Don't even rag on it. It's not like I'm thrilled about being the girl in some dumb rap video. I'm only doing it for the money. All I want is for Tristin to get off on my voice."

"Sure," Malshonda drawled sarcastically. "I believe you."

By the time Velvet was dressed and ready, it was late. Slick Jimmy was pleased to see her hit the set, but as Chanel was quick to point out, Slick Jimmy was pleased to see anything female. His group of overweight, sexy mamas were feeling the heat. They'd been at it all day. There was only so much booty to be jiggled and they were dragging. They lounged around in various stages of exhaustion, while Jimmy's CD blared over the loudspeakers.

Lousy lyrics, great beat, Velvet thought for the second time as she stepped in front of Malaki for his approval.

Malaki was not happy with her look, which immediately made her feel insecure. He requested further hair extensions, a more exotic makeup, and he wanted her dress to cling. Instead of shooting her piece, they rehearsed instead.

"You'll do your thing tomorrow," Malaki decided. "Tristin wants you perfect and so do I."

Hmm…Tristin wanted her perfect. That was interesting, especially coming from a man who until today had basically ignored her.

She'd been thinking about Chanel and her offer to set her up with a modeling agent. It sure beat the hell out of pouring coffee, so she thought she might ask her if she was serious. If it was a serious offer, she would definitely pursue it.

The time had come to take chances, and she was more than ready.

Chapter Six

Kareema had left a message on Famous's voicemail thatshe expected him to meet her at the airport.

Of course, she expected him to meet her. Kareema was used to getting everything her way. He went all out and hired a limo. Might as well pick herup in style.

When Kareema got off the plane, cleared Customs and began striding through Kennedy, clad in thigh-high leopard-print boots and a short, chocolate brown belted Prada raincoat, a couple of random photographers appeared out of nowhere and snapped her picture. They weren't certain who she was, but they quickly realized she was someone.

As soon as she saw Famous walking towards her, she threw out her arms and shouted, "Ciao, carino. It is somolto bene to see my boyfriend."

All of a sudden, he was her boyfriend? Well, yes, of course he was. They lived together, didn't they?

"Hey, baby," he said, hugging her. "You smell great."

"No, no, I smell of aero plane," she said, wrinkling her nose. "Is disgustoso, I need a shower."

"What hotel am I taking you to?" he asked, grabbing her Louis Vuitton carry-on bag, which weighed a ton.

"No hotel, carino, I'm staying with you," she said, tossing back her long hair.

This was a surprise, and not a welcomed one. How could he pursue a new relationship while Kareema was sharing his bed? "Well," he said slowly. "I kinda didn't ask Eddie if it—"

"Prego!" she explained. "Of course, Eddie invited me."

"Eddie doesn't know you," Famous pointed out.

"Ah, but if he did," she said, smiling knowingly, "You

certain he'd invite me?"

She was right, there wasn't a man in the world who would turn Kareema down.

He had to admit, she looked spectacular. Tall and slender, with a mane of auburn hair, cat-like eyes, and full, luscious lips. Men were stopping to stare as she sashayed past, like they couldn't quite believe such a magnificent creature existed. Kareema's looks were extremely feral.

"I'm not sure Eddie's apartment is fancy enough for you," he said, taking her arm. "There's hardly any space in the bathroom for your make-up and stuff. Plus, there's no magnifying mirror, and you know how you love your mirrors."

"What I need, carino, when I have you?" she said affectionately. "I've missed my Yankee boyfriend so, so much."

Yankee boyfriend? It was her new favorite expression. She'd learned it from her grandfather, a Second World War veteran, and Famous hated it.

"Hey, I've missed you too," he said, not really meaning it, because the girl whose name he didn't know was on his mind big-time.

"Have you been a bad boy?" Kareema teased.

"Only as bad as you," he retaliated.

"Ha! Incredibile! I see only one other guy. Mr. Lamborghini. And we like him, sì?"

"How is my favorite car?" he asked, as they made their way through the airport.

"I put in garage. Is bene, huh?"

"How long you staying?"

"We shoot photographs. We go home."

"Not we, you," he said quickly. "I have to stay around for a couple of weeks."

"Perchè?" she asked, disappointed.

"Because there's a few things I gotta take care ofbefore I can leave."

"Che cosa things?"

"Family stuff."

"You make Kareema triste."

"Sorry, baby. It can't be helped."

In the limo she hugged him again, her tongue snaking its way into his ear. "Kareema cannot wait to be alone with you," she whispered. "We make delizioso amore all night."

"Later tonight," he corrected. "Earlier we're invited to mybrother's rehearsal dinner."

"Che cosa rehearsal dinner?"

"Something people do before they get married."

"I thought that was sex," she said, her hand descending on, to his thigh.

"You think everything's sex."

"Is bene, no?" she said, with a husky laugh. "Not always."

"You like, you know you do," she cooed, her handmoving further up. "How they say in American? You are insatiable–sì?"

"Maybe we should wait until we get to the apartment," he said, deftly removing her hand. "There's a driver up front getting his rocks off watching our every move."

"So? That is bad?" she said, snuggling against his shoulder, her tongue once again flicking towards his ear.

And he realized there was no escaping Kareema.

***

Sunday noon, Carolyn Scott-Simon had arranged a major sit-down with Lynda Colefax, the wedding planner. She wished to make sure that all final details were in place since mishaps were not on her agenda.

Wandering around her mother's dining room, fervently wishing she was somewhere else, Shemika listened while the two women droned on about the usual subjects, flowers, seating, guests. It seemed their appetite for wedding trivia was never-ending.

"Shemika, will you kindly concentrate?" Carolyn scolded. "Who do you wish to sit at the head table?"

"Family, Mother." She sighed. "We've been over it ahundred times. Family, Megan and Tyrese."

"What about Alexia Ciccone and her escort?" Carolyn said. "Shouldn't they be at the head table?"

"I don't want them at the head table, Mother."

"Alexia Ciccone is your boss," Lynda pointed out, determined to be involved in every single decision. "Etiquette dictates—"

"I still don't want her at the head table," Shemika interrupted, wishing Lynda would butt out of stuff that was none of her business.

"Touch has still not told me if his father will be attending," Carolyn said irritably. "It's appallingly bad manners."

"Absolutely," agreed Lynda.

"I think he will be coming," Shemika offered. "He was at Touch's bachelor party. That's a good sign, isn't it?"

"It's not that I care whether he comes or not," Carolyn said snippily. "It's simply so rude not to reply. I should call Lady Bentley and ask her myself."

"Allow me to take care of it," said Lynda, jotting a reminder onto a large Gucci writing pad.

"No," Carolyn responded. "It's something I should deal with personally.

An hour later, Shemika was thrilled to get out of there. The wedding plans were making her dizzy. What a ridiculous fuss about one day.

She hailed a cab and was just about to give the driver her address when she made a spur-of-the-moment decision and instead gave him the address of her mystery man, an address that was somehow or other embedded in her brain.

Not that she planned on ringing his bell; she just thought she might take another look at the building where she'd spent the night and lost her virginity. Why not? She had nothing else to do.

***

Lady J continued putting her time alone to good use. If Red Bentley wished to treat her as if she was dispensable,she would do whatever it took to protect herself.

On Saturday night he did not come home, so on Sunday she resumed her investigation of his private domain, printing out several emails from Red to Patrick Sumter at the Magiriano Hotel in Las Vegas requesting that he pressure Krush to pay his debt, and other emails from the two banks Red, had forced to withdraw from Touch's building project.

She discovered nothing new about Famous, except a detailed report from the rehab clinic in Italy.

For a fleeting moment, she felt sorry for the three young men. Having Red as a father must have been a hideous experience. And yet they all managed to survive and do well. At least, two of them had. Who knew how Famous had turned out?

She had no idea why Red had summoned them to a meeting on Monday morning. He was probably going to inform them they were inheriting nothing, and because he was Red Bentley, he wanted to tell them personally. That way he could watch them cringe.

Red Bentley was exactly what everyone said he was. A true bastard.

**

Touch decided there was no way in hell he was giving Sadiya blood money to get rid of Draygo Kashif. If she swore to him that the marriage papers were fake, then he would take it up with the authorities and have Draygo deported. Yes, that was what he'd do. And by God, she'd better not be lying.

He went over to her apartment on Sunday morning. Irena, her personal maid, opened the door and let him in. "Is she around?" he asked.

"I get her," Irena muttered.

A few minutes later, Sadiya came into the living room. She seemed unusually pleasant and since this was not a happy occasion, he knew she must be up to something. "Do you have the money?" was the first thing she asked.

"I never agreed to bring money," he answered.

"Yes, you did," she said, the good mood quickly slipping away.

"No, I didn't," he said sharply. "Where's Camryn?" he added. He didn't want his little daughter overhearing their conversation.

"Out with her nanny."

"Let me explain why I'm here," he said, trying to keep his temper under control. "The next time Draygo comes to my office, I'm calling in detectives and having him arrested for extortion."

"You cannot do that," Sadiya argued, her demeanor turning positively icy.

"I can and I will," Touch said. "So, Sadiya, understand

that if you have anything to tell me, you should do it now."

"I can't believe you did not bring the money," she said, her face sulky. "You are so stupid. Things are already in motion."

"What things are in motion?" he asked, alarmed that she might have done something foolish.

"I need that cash. I have people to pay."

"For what?"

"Stop acting so innocent, Touch. You know what."

"No, Sadiya," he said harshly. "Whatever you've arranged, you must put a stop to it immediately."

"It's too late."

"It had better not be."

They stared at each other for a long moment, both busy with their own thoughts.

Finally, Touch broke the silence. "For God's sake, Sadiya, were you married to Draygo or not? I need to know the truth."

"You want the truth, I tell the truth," she said, practically spitting at him.

"Go ahead," he said, dreading what he was about to hear.

"Yes," she said, her voice rising. "I was married to Draygo. Does that make you happy?"

Touch felt his heart sink, furious that she'd just confirmed his worst fears. How could he have been married to this lying, conniving bitch?

"I came from poor family," Sadiya continued. "Moscow was hell-hole, I had to get out somehow."

"While we're on a truth kick, Sadiya, were you working as a prostitute too?"

"No!" she said, glaring at him. "How dare you think that?"

"Why shouldn't I? You've lied about everything else."

"You must understand, Touch, there was no choice for a beautiful woman other than to prostitute herself, but I never did that. When Draygo tried to force me to do certain things, I managed to escape and came to America."

"So, you and Draygo were never divorced?"

"If he'd suspected I was leaving—"

"This means that when you married the accountant, then me, both marriages were false? You committed a big sin, Sadiya?"

"Surely you now realize why we must get rid of him," she said bitterly.

"Jesus Christ, Sadiya. Why couldn't you have beentruthful with me before?"

"You left me, Touch," she said accusingly. "You left mealone."

"I did not leave you alone. I left you with a large financial settlement and the pleasure of raising our child."

"I will never forgive you for leaving me," she said, eyes glittering dangerously. "Now you're marrying this stupid girl. Everyone is laughing at you."

"You really are a piece of work," he said, still trying to control his temper. All he wanted to do was slap her until she cried out for mercy. He would never forgive her for what she'd done to Camryn. Never.

"Everywhere there are rumors," she continued. "I hear you are in financial trouble. How you think that makes me look?"

"That's all you're interested in, isn't it?" he said wearily. "The way you look."

"Appearances are important."

"You want to talk about appearances. Did you ever think about me and Camryn? Our marriage was a sham, and you know what that makes Camryn."

"With Draygo gone, nobody will ever know."

"You're fucking crazy."

"You will see, disposing of Draygo is our only answer."

"No, Sadiya. I'm having him arrested, and I don't give a damn what the newspapers say."

"You should, Touch, because it affects your daughter."

"Leave Camryn out of this. I've already spoken to my lawyers about gaining full custody."

"That will never happen."

"You want to bet?"

"You're a smart man, Touch, so listen carefully. Draygo will not be coming to your office again. I have taken care of the situation. And bring me cash, or there will be more problems to deal with. People perform services, they expect to get paid."

He stared at her in shock, realizing what she wasimplying.

She met his gaze, cool and composed.

And he knew, filled with dread, that maybe this time she was speaking the truth.

***

Huddled in the back of the cab across from the apartment where she'd spent her one wild night, Shemika began to feel like a stalker. What was she doing? Was she planning on getting out of the cab, going up to his apartment, knocking on his door, and saying, "Hi, I'm thegirl from the other night. Do you remember me?"

No, she wasn't doing that.

Then why was she here? It was stupid.

The cab driver had his radio on, Kid Rock was mumbling about kicking someone's ass.

"How long we gonna sit here, Miss?" the cab driver

asked, turning his head, and throwing her a squinty look.

"I'm, uh, waiting for somebody," she answered vaguely. "Five minutes or so. Is that okay?"

"You're paying," he said, picking up a copy of the New York Post and proceeding to read the sports pages.

Now what? She was here on a whim, and it was a total waste of time.

Just as she was about to tell the driver they could leave, a limo pulled into sight and stopped in front of the building.

She leaned forward, and sure enough there he was, Eddie Rogers getting out of the limo looking even more handsome than she remembered. He had on jeans, tennis shoes, and a denim work shir. His dirty blond hair was flopping on his forehead.

Should she get out of the cab and pretend she was just passing? Should she run over to him and say, 'Hi, I thought we should talk about what happened between us.' Or would a simple 'What's your name?' suffice?

Before she could decide what to do, he leaned down and began to help someone out of the limo. It turned out to be possibly one of the most beautiful women Shemika had ever seen.

She cringed against the back seat of the cab, holding her breath as she watched the beautiful woman throw her arms round his neck and kiss him. Long, lingering kisses.

He started laughing, while attempting to push her away in a *don't stop, I really like it,* fashion.

Was the woman his wife, girlfriend, what?

The driver of the limo opened the trunk and unloaded several Louis Vuitton suitcases, which he then lagged into the building.

And all the while the beautiful woman kept hugging Eddie Rogers and touching him in places Shemika didn't want to think about.

After a few minutes the two of them vanished inside, and she could finally breathe again.

"We can go now," she managed.

"Okay, where to?" asked the cab driver, throwing down his newspaper.

"Home," she said, in a small voice. "Where I belong."

Von Diesel

Chapter Seven

As soon as he saw his home in daylight, Krush realized exactly what a disaster area it was. His white house was buried under a huge amount of mud. Even worse, the structure looked like it was half collapsed, and a good partof it seemed about to teeter down the hillside.

The unexpected L.A. weather had demolished his home, and what could he do about it?

Exactly nothing.

There were certain things he could control, like his feelings about his father, the way he dealt with his clients, his love life, but not the weather.

He stood there in the driving rain staring at his once immaculate home for a long time, thinking about all the work he'd put into it, and everything he'd lost. His Cybex-equipped gym, his specially crafted pool table, his collection of rare movies on DVD, his multiple plasma TVs,everything he possessed.

This was an act of nature, and he wasn't sure if insurance covered natural disasters. Only this wasn't about the money, this was about losing his home.

Chi-rone met him there, then drove with him to LAX.

"You've got to get my safe out," Krush instructed him. "It is imperative that you do. And be sure to stay around when they dig it out. It's on your head if anything gets stolen."

"I won't leave the site," Chi-rone assured him. "I'll set upcamp in my car. No leaving until you tell me to."

"You're a good kid," Krush said, and decided that Chi-rone definitely deserved a raise.

Once he was settled in the airport lounge waiting to board his plane back to New York, he called the journalist

Damiun had entertained at his apartment. The man's name was Lionel Kemp, and Krush had checked him out on the internet. He was indeed a legitimate journalist working for *Sugar in My Tank* magazine, one of the better gay publications.

Krush introduced himself and told him how much he admired his work, especially the piece he'd written on homophobia in Hollywood.

Lionel seemed to enjoy the compliments, until Krush revealed he was Damiun Likely's lawyer. When Lionel heard that, he became verbally abusive, carrying on about movie stars who thought they owned the world.

Krush let him rant for a while, then hit him with the words every writer long to hear. "You're very talented, Mr. Kemp. Have you ever thought about writing a screenplay?"

Silence. Then, "Well, I do have some ideas…"

"Excellent. Because I'm ready to pay for those ideas."

Another, shorter silence. Then, "How much?"

Bingo! Everyone was for sale. All you had to do was establish a price.

***

It seemed to Famous that Kareema was being overly affectionate. He couldn't remember her ever being this clingy, she was all over him. Maybe America had this effect on her because the moment they entered Eddie's apartment, she was intent on making love. He demurred; he simply wasn't feeling like it.

"I take a shower, then we do it," Kareema announced, flouncing into the bathroom, shedding a trail of expensive clothes along the way.

When she emerged ten minutes later, there was no escape.

She strode toward him like a magnificent panther, sleek, naked, and ready for action.

Even though he wasn't in the mood, he was a man and automatically his dick jumped to attention.

She threw her arms around his neck and licked his face. "Ah, carino, I miss you," she whispered seductively. "You have everything Kareema likes."

Her hands were all over him, caressing his balls, stroking his cock, making him rock hard.

He couldn't resist her. They fell on top of the bed and began indulging in sexual acrobats, because that was what Kareema was into. She refused to lie there and allowa man to do what he had to do, she got her kicks taking control and giving him intense pleasure.

By the end of their lovemaking session, he felt more as if he'd experienced a vigorous workout. There was only one word to describe Kareema, and that was *predatory*. She was like an animal. She wanted to fuck, eat, and sleep, in that order.

She flopped on the bed, arms thrown above her head, long legs spread wide. "Kareema sleep now," she said, with a satisfied smile. "You wake me one hour before we go."

Once she was asleep, he started thinking about what his mom had told him about Krush paying for him to go to Italy and covered his treatment in rehab. How come his brother had never mentioned it? He'd always thought Eddie had paid for everything.

He called the Four Seasons. There was no answer from Krush's suite, so he tried Touch.

"Is Krush coming tonight?" he asked.

"He's on a plane back," Touch replied.

"Back from where?"

"He flew to L.A. There was an emergency, something to do with his house."

"You're kidding me?"

"No. There's devastating storms and rain hitting the coast. Seems his house was one of the casualties. He'll try to make it in time for dinner."

Even though he was somewhat in awe of Touch, this bonding between the three of them was kind of nice. Famous felt like he was part of a family, something he'd never experienced before. When he was growing up, Sukari had always been so busy with her drinking and her steady stream of younger boyfriends that she'd never had time for him. As for Red, well, the idea of Red as a father figure was one huge joke.

The moment Kareema awoke, she wanted to make love again. At twenty-four, Famous had plenty of stamina, so once more they went a few rounds. As far as he was concerned it was purely a physical thing. In his mind he was still thinking about the mystery girl and how he couldn't wait to see her again.

After their second vigorous lovemaking session, Kareema insisted on finishing him off with one of her spectacular blowjobs.

Man, she knew how to send a man flying and then some. Which was quite rare because beautiful women were usually not into giving head. Famous had always found they felt it was their right to receive, not give. Although with him, they usually changed their minds.

Finished with sex, Kareema began to unpack, flinging expensive clothes all over the bedroom, piling bottles and jars of make-up into the small bathroom, plugging her iPod speakers into the wall outlet so that her favorite Brazilian and Spanish music blared throughout the apartment. She was a big Marc Anthony and Carlos Santana fan and sang along at full volume. One talent Kareema did not have was singing.

"What I wear, carino?" she fretted, producing many elaborate designer outfits, and holding them up against her naked body.

"Dunno. Never been to one of these events," he said. "You'll look fantastic whatever you decide." "And you, what you wear?"

"I guess Levi's won't cut it, huh?" he said, pushing his hands through his hair and grinning.

"Prego," she said mischievously, fishing out a maroon plastic garment bag from her suitcase and handing it to him. "For you."

"What's this?" he asked, unzipping it.

"A gift from Mr. Armani," she replied with a jaunty wink as he extracted a sleek black Armani suit. "For my molto handsome Yankee boyfriend," she said, with a seductive smile. "Because he makes me very happy."

***

After a long, hot shower, Shemika felt she'd washed away all memories of her one night of craziness. She'd seen her mystery man in the light of day with another woman, the two of them affectionate and loving. That was enough for her. As far as she was concerned, it was over, a closed chapter, a memory she would try not to think about again.

She didn't regret it because it had made her realize that passion was a good thing, and she would find that same passion with Touch when they consummated their marriage. Actually, it was a relief because now she could concentrate on the rehearsal dinner and her husband-to-be. And she did love Touch. Megan was right, he'd be a perfect husband.

Impulsively, she picked up the phone and called him. "Just wanted to tell you how excited I am about tonight," she said softly.

"Hi, sweetie. How are you?" Touch responded, pleased to hear from her.

"Great, actually. The wedding meeting went well, and Mother was pleased."

"I'm glad for you. I know how difficult your mom can be."

"She's still wondering about your father. Have you any idea if he's coming or not?"

"I'll find out in the morning. That's a promise."

"Uh...Touch," Shemika said tentatively. "I'm sorry if I've seemed a bit edgy these last few days, but you know with the wedding coming up so soon and my mother driving me crazy, not to mention that bossy wedding planner, it's all been a bit of a strain."

"That's okay," he assured her. "I haven't been exactly calm myself."

"I know you didn't want to go through the ordeal of a rehearsal dinner," she continued, "but it is traditional, and it's for my mother, so having the dinner tonight really helps me out."

"I have no objections. Your mother organized every-thing, all I have to do is pay."

"Touch?"

"What now?"

"I love you," she said impulsively.

"You, too, sweetheart. See you soon."

She dressed slowly, taking her time. Vera Wang had de-signed a simple lilac silk dress for her. She added matching shoes, a discreet Bentley pendant, the tennis bracelet Grandma Poppy had given her, and a pair of diamond stud earrings, an earlier gift from Grandma Poppy.

When she was ready, she stood and stared at her reflection in the mirror.

Shemika Scott-Simon, soon to be Mrs. Touch Bentley. It would all work out.

***

On the plane back to New York, Krush was seated nextto a young actress he vaguely knew. Her name was Choosey Fallon, and she was overly talkative, which was exactly what he didn't need. They'd met once or twice when he was with Holly, and it was obvious she liked him or maybe she liked what he represented, a powerful L.A. entertainment lawyer. He could almost hear her mind ticking. *If I sleep with him, will he advise me for free?*

She informed him that she was flying to New York to appear on Letterman. Her latest movie, a horror flick, was about toopen, and she planned on doing a lot of promotion.

"Have you been on Letterman before?" he asked, attempting to be polite.

"No, but I heard he hates women," she confided. "ThenI heard he either hates them or flirts with them, so I'm gonna flirt. I'll wear something so low cut and sexy that he won't have a chance to be rude. And I'm told his studio is freezing, so my nipples will be very happy!"

"Shouldn't think you can outdo Drew Barrymore," Krush remarked.

"Why? What did she do?"

"Jumped on his desk, flashed her breasts in his face."

"I can do that," Choosey said, quite seriously.

"Do you want to?" he asked curiously.

"If it sells tickets, I'll do whatever it takes."

Actresses. They were all the same. Anything for attention.

Chandra was different. But Chandra wanted commitment, so now she was out. He hadn't bothered calling her in the short time he'd spent in L.A. Why even go there?

"Can I pick your brain?" Choosey asked, leaning close.

Sure, free advice, and she hasn't even fucked me. "Go ahead," he said.

"I've been offered two movies and I can't decide which to choose. One's with Denzel Washington, and the other is with Idris Elba. Who do you think is the hottest?"

So that's what it came down to. Who's the hottest? Not who's the most talented or who's got the best script? Just, who's the hottest? Pretty dumb. "I'd toss a coin," he said, feigning a yawn, hoping she might get the hint that he wanted to catch a nap. "Either way, you can't go wrong."

"Brilliant!" she said, a smile lighting up her ambitious face. "I never thought of that."

Earlier, he'd called Touch and told him he didn't think he could make it in time for the rehearsal dinner.

"I'd really appreciate you being here," Touch had said. "I want you to meet my fiancée. And who knows? Red might turn up again, which means I'll definitely need your support."

"Okay, I'll come straight from the airport," he'd promised. "Although, I'll probably be late."

"As long as you get here."

The flight attendant leaned down and whispered in Choosey's ear that Colin Farrell was on board. "He's traveling incognito," she said conspiratorially. "Sitting in the back of first class. I thought you'd be interested."

"Oooh," Choosey said, giggling at the thought of the adventure this might lead to. "Is anyone in the seat next to him?"

"No," the flight attendant assured her.

"Uh, excuse me," Choosey said to Krush. "Colin's an old friend. I'll be back in five minutes."

That was the last he saw of her, which didn't bother him at all. At least now he could get a few hours of sleep.

***

Sadiya was nowhere in sight when Touch arrived to collect Camryn to take her to the rehearsal dinner. Once more, Irena answered the door. He nodded at the overweight, frumpy woman, and asked her to fetch Camryn.

Seconds later, Camryn appeared dressed up in a pink party dress and happy as could be.

"Me going party, Daddy," she announced proudly. "Gonna see my uncles and Shemika, and all your friends."

"Yes, you are, sweetie," he said, bending down to give her a hug. "And you look so pretty."

"Mommy fixed my hair," she said, "Nice, Daddy?"

"Yes, Camryn, very nice."

"Can Mommy come too?"

"No, sweetie. Mommy is busy."

He managed to escape from the apartment without running into Sadiya. He'd already convinced himself that she was bluffing. There was nothing she could do about Draygo Kashif. She'd like to, but she wasn't capable of it.

"Camryn wants a present," Camryn announced in the elevator on their way down to the car.

"No, sweetie-pie, not tonight."

"Me want present," she said, pouting. "Daddy promised."

"I said not tonight, sweetie. You're coming to a very

grown-up dinner, and you're a lucky girl to be invited."

"Camryn wants a present," she repeated, her face suddenly crumbling, tears forming in her big blue eyes.

"No, Camryn," he said sternly.

"Camryn's tired." She sighed, lower lip trembling. "And hungry."

It suddenly occurred to him that Nanny Reece should be accompanying them. Why hadn't he thought of it before? Especially as Camryn was supposed to sleep overnight at his apartment.

As soon as they got out of the elevator, he hurried to the front desk and called upstairs. Nanny Reece answered the house phone. He informed her that she was to come with them, then reminded her that Camryn would be staying the night, and that she should be with her.

"Mrs. Bentley told me I could have the night off," Nanny Reece said, sounding irritated.

"Sorry, Nanny, you can't. I need you to be with Camryn. Mrs. Bentley should've told you."

"Very well, Mr. Bentley," Nanny Reece said. "I'll be down in five minutes."

Yes, he definitely should've thought about it before. In fact, Sadiya should've thought about it.

The truth was she probably didn't want him taking Nanny Reece because she relished the thought of Camryn jumping all over him so that he couldn't concentrate on his bride-to-be. A signature Sadiya move.

Yes. It crossed his mind for the thousandth time that divorcing Sadiya had been the best thing he'd ever done.

Chapter Eight

Sitting in the make-up chair on Sunday morning, Velvet decided she could easily get used to all the attention. She was getting the full-on glamour treatment, and she couldn't help liking it.

The hairdresser, a gay guy in a chartreuse tracksuit, brought in several falls to add to her hair. Chanel was busy contouring her face and applying false eyelashes one by one, while Fantasia made sure the scarlet dress fit her like second skin.

She knew she looked damn good. She also knew it wasn't her. It wasn't Velvet, the would-be singer-waitress. They'd turned her into some kind of amazing fantasy girl. But she had to admit, it *was* exciting.

When she hit the set, Malaki was all over her, calling her 'Sugar' and showing her exactly how he wanted her to slink around Slick Jimmy.

Slick Jimmy was all over her too. "You into anyone?" he asked, honoring her with a snaggled-tooth leer. "You and I should hook up 'cause *I'm* gonna be the *biggest*. Ya better catch me while ya can. All of them bitches and hoes gonna be *creaming* themselves over me."

"No, thanks," Velvet answered. "But if you ever need a back-up singer…"

"I be a rap artist, baby. *Rap*," he said, shooting her an angry glare. "Not one of them fancy soul singers like Brian McKnight or fucking Keith Sweat. I ain't down with *that* shit. This dude's *today!*"

"Lucky you," she murmured.

"You *dissing* me, girl?" he said, sweat beading his brow. 'Cause you do that and I'ma have your ass thrown off this motherfucking shoot. I don't give a fuck how fine you are."

"What's the deal with the sexist lyrics?" Velvet asked, ignoring his threat. "I'm sure you can write more original stuff."

"Fuck *you,*" he said, glaring at her. "Fat Girls gonna be the number-one song of the year, off the freaking *hook.* What you know about singing anyway?"

"It's what I do. I'm a singer, and I write my own songs."

"You recorded anything?" he said, staring at her with a challenging sneer.

"No, but Tristin Juzang wants to hear my stuff."

"Yeah, baby," Slick Jimmy said, with a full-on smirk. "He wants to get *into* your stuff, *that's what* the man wants."

Why was it that everybody was under the same impression? Because she looked good, was that what *everyone* thought?

The morning passed quickly. Malaki seemed happy with her interaction with Slick Jimmy. Much as she didn't like the rapper, she was getting into it by pretending it was a game. Acting, that was what it was.

At the lunch break, Tristin Juzang appeared.

She wasn't sure how to behave. Was she supposed to rush over and thank him? After all, he'd picked her out and was paying her all this money to appear in the video. According to Malaki via Chanel, he *liked* her. What exactly did that *mean?*

Then she thought, *no.* Kissing his ass like everyone else was not her style.

He was dressed casually in a cream-colored cashmere sweater, black pants and a New York Jets baseball cap worn backwards. Once more, everyone started fussing around him and making sure he had everything he needed. He accepted all the attention as if it was his due.

After a few minutes he and Malaki got into a conversation, and then the two of them strolled over to the video assistant so that Tristin could view what had already been shot.

"Go say hi," Malshonda urged, nudging her. "Go *on*."

"Why would I do that?"

"Because he *likes* you, and you *like* him," Malshonda teased.

"No, I *don't*," she said crossly, wishing she hadn't passed on that piece of information to Malshonda. "How many times do I have to tell you? All I need from him is to listen to my demo. Besides, if he wants to speak to me, he can come over here."

"Oooh, Miss Playing It Cool," Malshonda taunted. "Get *you*."

Malshonda's words didn't faze her. She'd made her decision and she was sticking to it.

The assistant director had assigned her a director's chair, and she walked over and sat in it.

Malshonda trotted after her. "I'm gonna grab me some lunch at the catering truck," she announced, clutching a flimsy wrap around her bountiful curves. "You coming?"

"This dress is so tight, I can't eat," Velvet said.

"Want me to bring you something?"

"I'm not hungry. Think I'll stay here."

"Sure, *starve* yourself to death," Malshonda said, taking off.

Somebody had left a copy of *People* magazine lying around, Velvet picked it up and began leafing through it.

A few moments later, he was standing next to her. She knew he was there because she could smell his very expensive, very distinctive, masculine cologne. She forced herself not to look up.

"Hey," he said, tapping her shoulder. "Thought I'd be

receiving a very big thank-you right about now."

She glanced up. "Mr. Juzang," she said, feigning surprise. "Of course, I thank you, only this is not what I do. It's an experience, that's all. Oh yes, and I do appreciate the money."

"Something is different about you," he said, raising his tinted shades and squinting at her.

"Good or bad?" she responded, putting down the magazine.

"You were a beauty before," he observed. "Now you're really styling."

"Thanks, Mr. Juzang." And she wanted to add, *How come you never noticed me when I was serving you coffee every morning? What was I, invisible?*

"Think you'd better call me Tristin," he said, giving her a long, lazy stare. "Gotta hunch we're gonna be tight."

Trying to ignore his incredibly sexy eyes, she stayed on the subject of her music. "I brought my demo with me today. I'd like to play it for you."

"You would, huh?" he said, not taking his eyes off her.

"Yes, I would," she said, still pretending not to notice his intense scrutiny.

"So...Velvet," he said, rubbing his slightly stubbled chin with his index finger, "you're serious? You *are* a singer."

"Did you think I was making it up?"

"Who knows today? Everyone's chasing a piece of the action."

"Then how come you sound surprised?"

"You know," he said, suddenly serious, "Straight singers ain't my deal. I'm in the hip-hop, rap business."

"No," she corrected. "You're in the *record* business, you can *deal* with who you like."

"I can?"

"You're the boss, aren't you?"

"Yeah," he agreed, with an amused grin. "I'm the boss."

"If you can't listen to my demo now, can I come to your

office tomorrow and you'll listen to it then?"

"Got no reason to stop you."

"What time?" she asked, determined to pin him down.

"You could show up around six-thirty."

"I'll be there."

"And, uh...Velvet—"

"Yes?"

"Keep it between us," he said, then walked away.

Chanel was right, he was definitely coming onto her. Not that he'd actually *said* anything. It was all in his eyes, those smoky incredibly sexy eyes.

And yet, if he *was* on the make, how come he'd walked away? And what was with the "keep it between us"? Like, *who* was she going to tell?

Hmm...He was into game-playing. Yes, that was it.

Well, she might not be in his league, but she knew how to play a game or two herself.

And the best news of all was that she had an appointment with him tomorrow, six-thirty, at his office.

And she *would* be there. Because Tristin Juzang was her one big shot at the future.

Von Diesel

Chapter Nine

The rehearsal dinner was being held at the Waldorf Astoria to accommodate Grandma Poppy. She was ninety years old, so having dinner at her residence hotel made it easier for her.

Shemika arrived early and took the elevator upstairs to fetch her. "Hi, Grams," she said, kissing her adored grandmother on both cheeks. "Don't *you* look lovely?"

"Thank you, dear."

"You're *sure* you're up to this?" Shemika asked, concerned that it might be too much for the old lady.

"Wouldn't miss your party," Grandma Poppy said, fiddling in a beaded bag. "The moment I've had enough, Hueng will bring me back upstairs."

"Then you'd better be sure you tell him when you're ready," Shemika said sternly. "No overdoing it."

"Allow me to look at you, child," Grandma Poppy said. Shemika executed a little twirl, showing off her dress. "Delightful!" Grandma Poppy exclaimed. "I'm *so* proud of you, dear. I do hope your young man appreciates the prize he's getting."

"He's not so young, Grams," Shemika said, with a faint smile. "Touch is in his forties."

"That's young, dear."

Hmm…Shemika thought. *Anyone under seventy is probably young to Grams*. "Shall we go downstairs?" she asked. "Are you ready?"

"In a minute," Grandma Poppy replied, fishing an old leather ring box out of her bag, and handing it to her granddaughter. "First, I have something for you."

Shemika accepted the gift and opened the box. Inside was an antique emerald ring, with Bentleys and tiny pearls. "Grams, this is exquisite," she gasped. "Are you absolutely *sure* you want to give it to me?"

"It was a present from an Indian prince when I was a mere girl," Grandma Poppy said, a faraway look in her eyes. "He promised it would bring me a long life andhappiness. It seems he was right, so now I bestow those precious gifts on you."

"Thank you *so* much," Shemika said, slipping the ring on her finger. "I couldn't love it more."

"I'm ready to go," Grandma Poppy said crisply. "I refuse to miss one moment of this extremely important occasion. Come along, dear. It's time we started celebrating."

***

"How I look?" Kareema asked, knowing full well she looked incredible.

"Not bad," Famous replied, provoking her.

"Scusi!" she exploded, not taking him seriously at all.

"Bastardo!" They both began to laugh.

He couldn't wait to see the expressions on his brothers' faces when they got an eyeful of Kareema. She was featuring her Italian supermodel look, a Roberto Cavalli outfit that was totally wild. It consisted of a long, gypsy-style skirt, a suede and leather-studded vest worn over a skimpy python-print bra, multiple ivory and gold crosses strung around her swan-like neck, plus fourteen ivory and silver bangles graced her wrist. There was plenty of toned, taut skin on display.

So what? Famous thought. *Give the New York natives a show.*

He was wearing his new Armani suit, which fitted him perfectly, and a black silk shirt unbuttoned at the collar. They made a striking couple.

Famous wondered if there was any way he could palm

off Kareema on Krush. His brother had told him he was breaking up with his current girlfriend, so why not? Kareema was the perfect girl to help a man get over a break-up. She was a fun-loving, sex-mad goddess. What more could any man ask for?

"Come on," he said, dragging her away from the mirror and out of the apartment. As they crowded into the tiny elevator he said, "Did I tell you about my brother, Krush? He's a major entertainment lawyer in Hollywood. Looks after all kinds of stars, Chilly Rose, Damiun Likely."

"I like, how do you say? Jamie Foxx," Kareema said,licking her lips. "Very sexy, no?"

"Don't think he's Krush's client. But hey, have you ever thought of moving into acting?"

"*Scusi?*"

"Maybe you should talk to Krush about it. I'm sure he could hook you up." "S*i?*" Kareema said, not particularly interested.

"Yeah, really," Famous said, pushing it. "You know, a lot of actresses start out as models. Cameron Diaz is example number one."

"Cameron *who?*"

"Diaz. She's big in America. Look, I'll make sure you get a chance to talk to Krush tonight. Could be the start of something."

***

Lady J Bentley was on a mission, and that mission was to gain entry to Red Bentley's safe. All she needed was the combination and knowing Red, he would have written it down somewhere.

As she continued her thorough search, she couldn't help recalling their first meeting. He'd lured her into his bed with lavish gifts and promises of what she would get if she left her husband and moved in with him. At the time, she was married to one of his business rivals, Lord James Donovan, an English media tycoon whom Red loathed.

When it came to the pursuit of a business he wished to acquire or a woman he wanted, Red Bentley was ruthless. It had taken him many months, but eventually he'd won her over. She left her husband, and moved back to America to be with Red.

The headlines were lurid. There was nothing like a good juicy scandal in Billionaire Land. And Red was triumphant. As usual, he'd won.

At first, Lady J had been fascinated by Red Bentley. His very ruthlessness was an aphrodisiac, not to mention his vast fortune, plus he was a ferocious lover. She also preferred New York to London, it was more exciting. Moving back, she'd been looking forward to entertaining on a grand scale. However, after a while, she realized Red Bentley was not the man that she'd left her husband for. He was a cruel tyrant, who cared about nobody but himself. He had no desire to entertain, no wish to travel, he was estranged from his three sons, and he hardly ever left his house. The lovemaking stopped as soon as she was in residence. All he required was that she serve him orally twice a day, a sexual act she considered repugnant and demeaning.

Lady J found herself in an impossible position. She'd left her husband to be with Red in such a public fashion that it would be a major embarrassment to admit defeat. She had chosen to ignore Red's shortcomings and made a life with him. Because, honestly, how much longer did he have? After all, she was thirty years younger than him and could afford to wait.

When she'd first moved in, he'd assured her that she was well taken care of in his will. What exactly did that mean?

And now that he was telling her to get out, how did that affect her position?

It was imperative that she find his will so that she could see for herself exactly what it said.

Since he had failed to return home on Saturday night, she had had plenty of time to conduct an even more thorough search of his personal papers.

At six o'clock on Sunday night she had discovered the entry code to his personal safe written on a packet of book matches hidden in the inside pocket of one of his suits. It was a satisfying moment for she knew she had discovered the gateway to all his secrets.

Camryn was the only child at the rehearsal dinner, so everyone was oohing and aahing about how adorable she was. Everyone except Carolyn Scott-Simon, who was not happy that her future son-in-law already had a child with some dreadful foreign woman who was known in New York society to be a relentless social-climber. Carolyn would have preferred her only daughter to be marrying a man *without* baggage. But at least Touch Bentley was rich, and could support Shemika without expecting her to contribute. Young, pretty heiresses had to be extremely careful, fortune-hunters lurked round every corner. And Shemika wasn't the most stable girl, she needed a man who would assume control.

Shemika led Grandma Poppy over to Touch. "You remember Grams," she said, holding onto her grandmother's frail arm.

Checking out his bride-to-be, Touch couldn't get over what a lucky man he was. Shemika was a vision of perfection in her pale lilac dress, with her natural blonde hair half up and half down, wearing exactly the right amount of jewelry. Shemika Scott-Simon was a class act. A world apart from Sadiya. "Of course, I do," he said, bending down to kiss the old lady's cheek. "How are you, Grandma?"

"I'm not *your* grandma, young man," Grandma Poppy said, giving him a withering look. "*You* may call me Poppy."

"I'll be happy to," Touch said, suitably deflated.

"I'd like Grams to meet Camryn," Shemika said quickly. "Where is she?"

"Over there in the middle of an admiring crowd," Touch said, waving across the room.

"I do hope she has a nice time tonight," Shemika said, thinking it wouldn't be pleasant if Touch's little girl threw one of her tantrums.

"I'm sure she'll behave," Touch assured her, "and if she doesn't, too bad. This is *our* night, sweetheart. Nobody can spoil it."

"It certainly is," she answered warmly. "Oh, there's Megan. I should run over and say hello. Grams, would you like to come with me?"

"No, thank you," Grandma Poppy said grandly. "Lead me to my seat and I will allow people to come to *me*. I won't trail behind you all night as if I am an ancient appendage!"

Shemika glanced around, searching for her mother. As soon as she saw her, she took Grandma Poppy over and settled her at the main table, with Hueng in attendance, then made her way over to Megan and Tyrese's table where they were about to sit down with a group of her friends from work. Sassy, Chinky and Milly had all brought dates, while Nigel was with his significant other, the languid Marcello, who, much to Nigel's annoyance seemed quite taken with Sassy's date, a barely legal toy-boy.

Shemika wished she was sitting at their table: she knew they were all set to have a great time. Rehearsal dinners were far less formal than actual weddings, and now that she was over her mystery man, she was determined to enjoy herself. She wanted Touch to do the same. He had to stop worrying and let himself go for once.

"You okay?" Megan asked, her stomach bulging out of a blue satin dress that appeared to be bursting at the seams.

"*You*'re the one about to give birth," Shemika replied.

"Not tonight, I hope," Megan responded, patting her huge belly.

"Let us pray," said Tyrese, Megan's stockbrokerhusband, rolling his eyes.

"Soon as I can, I'll be back to sit with you," Shemikapromised. "Your table is definitely the most fun."

"That's if I don't give birth," Megan joked. "What, and ruin my party?" Shemika quipped.Everyone laughed.

"Ve*ry* stylish," Milly said admiringly, fingering thematerial of Shemika's dress.

"Vera Wang," Nigel said. "Made especially for little missy."

"Yeah, well, *little* missy better not let *big* missy Cicconefind out," Sassy said. "Lucky she's not here tonight."

Shemika was already hurrying back across the room to Touch.

"Good job. I brought the nanny," Touch said. "Otherwise,I'd be stuck worrying about the kid all night. You know how she can get."

"Not *stuck* with her, Touch," Shemika corrected gently. "She's your daughter."

"She'll be *our* daughter soon."

"No," Shemika said. "I'll be her step-mom. She already *has* a mother."

"You're sure that taking on a ready-made family is okay with you?" he asked, scratching his chin.

"One little girl is hardly a ready-made family," Shemi-kasaid, smiling softly. "Besides, we'll have our own children one day."

"That's right," he said. "I was thinking a boy and a girl."

"You can't order what you want,Touch," she teased.

"Oh, no? Because I read there are ways of deciding."

"Where did you read *that*?"

"Apparently, you stand on your head for a girl or hangout of the window for a boy."

Shemika began to laugh. "You're funny when you talklike that."

"I am?"

"Yes, and you're usually so serious."

"Guess I've been mixing with my brothers too much," he said wryly. "I hope you like them."

"I can't wait to meet them. Where are they?"

"Krush is coming straight from the airport and, bigsurprise, Famous is running late."

"Is that his reputation?"

"Excuse me?"

"Always late."

"Famous has a far bigger reputation than that."

"He does?"

"I should warn you that he seems to have cleaned himself up, but a few years ago, he was heavily into drugs."

"That's a shame."

"Yes, it is, but in a way it's understandable. Red was a hard taskmaster and none of us had it easy, but Famous being the youngest, got the brunt."

"So, once again, it's all your father's fault?"

"You could say that."

"He sounds like a dreadful man."

"Believe me, he is."

"What's Krush like?"

"Smart, easy-going. You'll enjoy his company."

Impulsively, Shemika leaned over and kissed her future husband's cheek.

"What's *that* for?" Touch asked.

"Just for nothing," she said, once more smiling softly.

***

As the guests began finding their appointed tables and sitting down for dinner, Famous arrived with Kareema at his side. They didn't so much arrive, as they made an entrance. A big entrance.

Reactions were mixed.

"Who on *earth* is *that?*" Carolyn Scott-Simon demanded of Lynda Colefax, who had no idea. She turned to Shemika to find out, but Shemika had gone to the ladies' room.

"What a divine creature," Grandma Poppy murmured, observing Kareema. "I can see she is a free spirit, exactly like I used to be when *I* was a young girl."

Across the room, Tyrese nudged Megan. "Who's the babe?" he asked.

"Stop looking!" Megan said crossly, slapping his wrist. "You have a pregnant *wife*! Keep your lecherous eyes to yourself."

"It's the Italian supermodel, Kareema," Nigel said, totally in awe. "She's in town to appear in our new ad campaign."

"Never mind the girl," Sassy said, fanning herself with a napkin. "Feast your eyes on the hottie she's with. Now *he* can join me in my bed *anytime*."

"Ve*ry* sexy," murmured Marcello, causing Nigel to fix him with a jealous glare.

"He looks sort of familiar," Megan said, peering across

the room. "Wasn't he—"

"I think *he*'s a model too," Nigel said, always a fountain of information. "I'm sure I've seen his picture in Italian *Vogue*."

"I wonder what they're doing *here?*" Megan said.

"Perhaps they're friends of Touch's," Nigel suggested.

While everyone stared, Touch stood up and went over to greet his brother and girlfriend.

"Touch," Famous said, loosening his collar. "Meet Kareema. Kareema, this is my big brother, Touch."

Before Touch could say a word, Kareema flung her arms round him, kissing him on both cheeks. "Soon you will be married," she gushed. "*Molto bene. Salutations.*"

"Thank you," Touch said, taking a step back, her rich, musky perfume overwhelming him.

"Where is your bride? I must say *ciao*," Kareema said, the ivory and silver bracelets jangling half-way up her tanned bare arms.

"Here she comes now," Touch said, relieved to see Shemika approaching.

Kareema turned around, so did Famous.

And there she was. Shemika. Cool and pretty. Walking towards them. A smile on her face until she spotted Famous standing with the beautiful woman from outside his apartment.

Her smile froze. *What was going on? Why were they here? Had Touch found out and was this his revenge?*

Oh, God! She wished she could close her eyes, open them, and find this was all an out-of-control nightmare.

But she couldn't. This was real, and she was totally helpless.

"Sweetheart," Touch said, seemingly unperturbed. "This is my brother, Famous, and his girlfriend, Kareema.

Famous, say hello to Shemika, my fiancée."

Shemika felt faint. Was this some kind of sick joke? His brother. Touch's *brother.*

No. It wasn't possible.

And how could he be called Famous? His name was Scott or Sonny or Simon. S. Lucas, that was who he was.

This couldn't be happening!

Before she could think straight, the woman was enveloping her in a hug, offering congratulations in a mixture of broken English and fluent Italian.

Then it was Famous's turn. She could read the shock in his eyes. Obviously, this was a surprise to him also.

He proffered his hand, acting as if they'd never met, which, of course, was the only sane way to play it.

She took his hand, shook it, and a jolt of pure electricity coursed through her body.

"You Americans!" Kareema exclaimed, with a husky laugh. "So *uptight.* Kiss the girl, *carino.* Soon, she will be part of your family."

Stunned, Famous withdrew his hand, and at that exact moment Camryn raced over, throwing herself into his arms. "Camryn's uncle," she chanted. "Uncle! Uncle! *Uncle!*"

He swung the little girl round, grateful for the diversion because he, too, was in deep shock.

"So *dolce!*" Kareema said, smiling agreeably at Touch. "Is yours?"

"Yes, she's mine," he answered proudly. "My little Camryn."

"You are *very* lucky man," Kareema said, and turned to include Shemika. "You will find much *amore* and happiness together."

What is she, a witch? Shemika thought. *A witch with the best body I've ever seen.*

I hate her.

No, I don't. It's not her fault. She probably has no clue that her boyfriend is a cheat.

"Let's all sit down," Touch suggested. "I can see your mother is getting agitated."

Camryn was still clinging to Famous. He carried the little girl to the table. "Me sit next to *you*," Camryn said, fluttering her long eyelashes at him.

"Sure, honey," he said, shooting a covert glance at Shemika, who looked even more lovely than he remembered. That gorgeous face. Those wide, innocent eyes. Her silky hair and glowing skin.

I'm in love, he thought. *I'm in love with my brother's fiancée. And what the hell am I supposed to do about that?*

Chapter Ten

By the time Krush arrived at the rehearsal dinner, thingswere in full swing. Harold was in the middle of making a heartfelt speech about his stepdaughter, of whom he was very fond, while the main course of steak and lobster had just been served.

"Over here," Touch called out, waving him to the table.

Krush slid quietly into the seat between Nancy's best friend, and Kareema, who turned to him with an animated expression and exclaimed in a loud whisper, "I *love* your brother. You and Ibe *bene bene* friends, *capisce?*"

So, this was the fabulous Kareema, she of the famous blowjobs and proud Lamborghini owner. "Sure," Krushsaid, thinking that Famous was one lucky baby brother.

On the way in from the airport, he'd called Damiun and told him everything was taken care of. "It'll cost you seventy-five grand and he'll sign a non-disclosure contract, which is being couriered to him now."

"You're the best!" Damiun had exclaimed, sounding suitably grateful. "Anything I can do for you, Krush, anything at all, never hesitate to ask."

Harold finished his speech to much applause. Touch immediately leaned across the table and introduced Krush to Shemika. Krush was impressed. It seemed that both of his brothers had done well for themselves in the girlfriend department.

"I gotta hit men's room," Famous said, standing up. "Comewith, Krush."

"That's okay, I don't—"

"I *need* to talk to you," Famous said, throwing him a meaningful look.

"Sure," Krush said, pushing his chair away from the table. "What's up?" he asked, as they headed for the men's room.

"What's up?" Famous repeated, groping for a cigarette in his jacket pocket.

"What's freaking *up*? That girl in there, that gorgeous incredible girl, Kareema?" Krush interrupted.

"No, not freaking Kareema," Famous snapped, confused, and frustrated. "Shemika, Touch's fiancée."

"What about her?" Krush asked, wondering what he was missing.

"She's *my* girl, *the* girl," Famous said, his hand shaking slightly as he lit his cigarette. "The one I've been trying to find."

"You're *not* telling me—"

"Yeah," Famous said grimly. "That's *exactly* what I'm telling you."

"Jesus *Krush*!" Krush exclaimed. "You *screwed* Touch's fiancée? *She*'s the one?"

"What the *fuck* am I gonna do?" Famous demanded, exhaling smoke.

Krush had no idea what Famous expected him to say. "Are you *sure* it's her?" he asked.

"C'*mon*, Krush," Famous said, shooting his brother a dirty look. "I'm not crazy. *Of course,* it's her."

"Has she said anything to you?"

"How can she? She's sitting right next to Touch, andshe's surrounded by her family."

"Jeez, do you think she *knew* you were Touch's brother when she went home with you?"

"No way. I mean, why the hell would she sleep with her fiancé's brother? What kind of a fucked-up deal is *that*?"

"Here's my question. Why would she sleep with *anyone* when she's about to get married?"

"Yeah," Famous said, "that's exactly what I keep asking myself."

"There's no way you can tell him," Krush said, imagining the consequences of Touch finding out. "Don't even consider it."

"Like I'd do that."

"Here's what you've got to do. Suck it up, forget it ever happened. Move on."

"Easy for you to say," Famous said miserably. "Only it *did* happen, and she's not a girl I can forget."

"Then, little bro', you'd better start trying. And my suggestion is that you do *not* mention this to anyone else. Keep it between us and we'll figure something out."

"I need a drink," Famous muttered.

"No," Krush said, knowing how impossible it would be if Famous were to get drunk. "That's exactly what you *don't* need."

"I can handle it."

"Getting shit-faced is a dumb move, Famous."

"So *what?* You think I can go back in there stone-cold sober?"

"If you plan on making it through the night."

"You're a big fucking help," Famous muttered.

"Just watching out for you, surfer kid."

"Yeah," Famous said wryly. "I guess you're getting good at that."

***

Back at the party they were showing a slide show of Shemika and Touch's childhood photos. There was Shemika aged two, naked and curly-haired, lying on a fur rug. Touch aged four, all dressed up in a grown-up suit, solemnly saluting. Shemika, five and adorable. Touch, ten and stern. Shemika at her junior prom and Touch at his. And so on...

Shemika could barely concentrate, her mind was racingin a hundred different directions. She kept glancing at Touch, making sure he hadn't set this up to punish and humiliate her.

No. It was just one of those things. An error of judgement. *Her* error.

Kareema was busy charming everyone, speakingnon-stop to anyone who would listen. She'd already bonded with Grandma Poppy, who pronounced her an absolute delight.

Finally, Krush and Famous returned to the table.

Shemika wondered if Famous had confided in his brother. Had he revealed the horrible truth? And would his next move be to tell Touch?

Oh, God! Maybe *she* should get to Touch before *he* did and confess everything.

For a fleeting second, her eyes met Famous's. Quickly, she looked away. What must he think of her?

As soon as she felt she could, she made a mad dash across the room to Megan's table, ready to divulge everything to her best friend and beg for her counsel because there was no way she could handle this by herself. Her stomach was churning, she felt totally shaky. What was she going to *do?*

When she reached Megan's table, some sort of commotion was taking place.

"Thank *God*!" Tyrese exclaimed, grabbing her by the shoulders. "For Christ sakes, Megan's gone into labor!"

"*What?*" Shemika cried out.

And from there it was, all one big blur as Shemikaelected to go with Megan and Tyrese to the hospital.

As soon as Carolyn found out, she was livid. "Youcannot

leave your own rehearsal dinner," she fumed. "I will not allow it."

"Sorry," Shemika yelled, as she assisted Megan past the main table. "This is my best friend, and she needs me."

"Go!" Touch said encouragingly. "I know how important this is to you, sweetie. Take the car, my driver's downstairs."

Oh, great! Now, he was being understanding and selfless. She wished he would scream and act like a man betrayed. She deserved it. Only he couldn't do that, could he? *Because he didn't know.*

She caught another brief glimpse of Famous. He was staring at her. She pretended not to notice.

"Stop!" Megan yelled, as they reached the door. "I think my water is breaking."

"Oh my God!" exclaimed Tyrese, starting to panic. "You can't give birth to our baby here!"

"I'll have our baby wherever I damn well please!" shouted Megan. "Go find the car, you idiot. Don't youunderstand? WE'RE HAVING A BABY!"

***

So that was it. There one minute, gone the next. And he hadn't even had a chance to say a word to her.

Shemika Scott-Simon.He knew her name.

A rich girl, so her mother's best friend, a skeleton on stick legs in an Oscar de la Renta fancy suit, had informed him. "When Grandma goes, the will bypasses Carolyn and Shemika inherits everything," the woman had confided in a stage-whisper. "We're all so happy that Touch is obviously not a fortune hunter. They make a delightful couple. Don't you agree?"

No. He didn't agree. Touch was too old for her. And who

gave a fast crap if she had money or not?

He'd fallen for a girl. A girl without a name or pedigree. An incredible girl with soft golden hair, an amazing body, and the face of an angel. And there was nothing he could do about it except sit back and watch.

Touch was beaming, even though Shemika had run off with her pregnant friend, which proved she was a loyal and decent person. The birth of her best friend's baby before rehearsal dinner. Good for her.

Shemika Scott-Simon.

Even her name had a ring to it.

Kareema was swigging champagne like it was going out of style. She enjoyed being the center of attention. Touch was obviously enjoying her, too, as she laughed and flirted with him. Famous was well aware that it was just Kareema's affectionate Italian ways. She was a very touchy-feely person, who got her kicks telling men how handsome and virile they were, making them feel good about them-selves. And if they fell in love with her, all the better.

Camryn had decided he was her favorite uncle and kept crawling onto his knee and locking her arms round his neck. He didn't object, she was so cute.

"Can Camryn come live with you?" she asked, all bright eyes and puffy lips.

"No, baby, you have a daddy and a mommy," he said, somewhat distracted. "You're very happy at home."

"Not happy," she said, vigorously shaking her head.

"Huh?" he said vaguely.

"My mommy's divorcing my daddy 'cause *he* doesn't like her," Camryn said, blinking several times. "That makes Camryn sad."

"Hey, sugar cake, I'm sure it's not as simple as that."

"It is," Camryn said stubbornly. "Daddy likes stupid

Shemika."

"Don't say that about Shemika."

"Why?" she asked, pulling a face. "Mommy says it."

"Because it's not true. Shemika's a great girl."

"No," Camryn cried. "Shemika stupid! Stupid! *Stupid!*"

The skeleton decided to find out more about Famous. "And what do *you* do?" she asked, tapping talon-like fingernails on the table. "Are you in the same business as your brother?"

"No, I'm uh..." He knew that once he said he was amale model, she would dismiss him on the spot. "I...I kinda work in fashion."

"How *divine*," she gushed. "Valentino is a dear friend. I adore his clothes, don't you?"

It was obvious that now she assumed he was gay.

He wondered if he could sneak a drink without Krush noticing. Then the voice of his sponsor in Italy came back to haunt him. *Remember, booze doesn't solve anything. It only makes things worse.*

"Krush," he said, touching his brother's shoulder. "I gotta get out of here. I cannot take much more of this."

"Don't blame you," Krush responded. "Uh...before I go, I wanted to thank you."

"For what?"

"I talked to Sukari earlier. She let it slip that it was *you* who sponsored my trip to Italy and got me out of the craphole I was in. I always thought it was Eddie. You did me a big favor because I don't know how many more ledges, I would've stood on thinking wouldn't it be fun to fly. You saved me from finding out."

"No need to thank me," Krush said, slightlyembarrassed. "You're my kid brother. We share a father, bad as he might be."

"Yeah." Famous laughed ruefully. "We grew up with the same beatings and the same favorite rants, 'you're useless, you're ugly, you're dumb, you'll never amount to anything'."

"I remember all of them," Krush said. "It's amazing we survived."

"Well, we did, so fuck him."

"Now, I'm wondering what the old bastard is going to sayin the morning."

"Who gives a shit?" Famous said. "At least we got tohang out this weekend."

"Makes this trip worth it for me," Krush agreed. "Andtomorrow, I'll tell you about my problems."

"You got problems too?"

"Major."

"Wanna share?"

"You sure?"

"Go ahead," Famous said, thinking they couldn't be any worse than his.

"Well…I have one famous client who thinks the public is about to discover he's gay, another client who's all set to marry some low-down wife-beater, and here's the *real* kicker, I lost my house."

"What do you mean, you *lost* your house?"

"You were right about the storms in L.A. People aregetting killed, mudslides, floods, it's a real mess."

"You *lost* your fucking house, and you're only telling menow?"

"Nothing you could do."

"Except be there for you."

"And you are."

"No, I'm not. I'm busy bitching about *my* life, while youlost your house. I'm sorry, man, I really am."

"Yeah," Krush said ruefully. "I'm kinda sorry myself. Buthey, keeps you grounded."

"You *sure* there's nothing I can do?"

"We should get together for an early breakfast before we meet Red tomorrow."

"I'm there," Famous said. "Your hotel?"

Krush nodded. "And for now, what can I say? We'll talk about everything in the morning."

"Thanks, bro'," Famous said, leaning over to tap Kareema on her shoulder. "We're outta here."

"Why we leave?" she asked, turning to him with a disappointed expression. Attention was like an aphrodisiac to the Italian supermodel, and tonight she was basking in it.

"Cause it's late, and you're in a different time zone."

"No, *carino*, we stay," she said firmly. "Your brother, heneeds us. We cannot desert him."

Oh yeah, this was all he needed. The bonding of Kareema and Touch. One big happy family. *Great!*

"We can't huh?" he said wearily. "Why the fuck not?"

And while the rehearsal dinner was taking place, and Red had *still* not returned home, Lady J opened his safe. She studied his will and several other private documents. Red's will was dated six months previously, and witnessed by two of his top executives.

She read everything and the color drained from her face.

Red Bentley was even more of a devious bastard than even *she'd* imagined.

The information she discovered was quite unbelievable, and yet…she should have known.

Damn him. Damn him to hell and back.

Von Diesel

Chapter Eleven

The girls were working hard, Malshonda still shaking her ass, Velvet draping herself over Slick Jimmy for the cameras.

It wasn't as easy as it looked. Slick Jimmy was not as polished with lip-synching, so they had to keep repeating take after take until he got it right. He'd also stopped talking to Velvet because, in his eyes, she wasn't being respectful to his music.

As if she cared. She had an appointment to play her demo for Tristin. Nothing could be better than *that*.

"We scored an invite to the wrap party," Malshonda confided during one of the numerous breaks.

"I thought we were dropping by your mom's."

"Mom's first, party later," Malshonda said, with a big grin. "It's gonna be lit."

"I'm not in the mood for a party," Velvet said.

"Oh, *c'mon*," Malshonda scolded. "Tomorrow it's back to *real* work, and all this will seem like a freaking *dream*. So tonight, we're getting *down*, girl, make *no* mistake."

Velvet frowned. She had no desire to get down. Thinking about returning to her job at the coffee shop was depressing enough. How could she possibly waitress for Tristin now? It didn't seem right. "I'm not going into work tomorrow," she informed Malshonda.

"How come?"

"Cause I'm not ready."

"Oh, *I* get why you don't wanna come in," Malshonda taunted knowingly.

"Because of Mr. Bigshot Tristin himself."

"That's not true."

"I'm telling you, girl, you'd better remember that working in the coffee shop is what we *do*. It's *real*. This shit *ain't*."

"You seem to forget I was hurt on the job," Velvet reminded her. "That means I can take a couple of days off. They should understand."

"Okay," Malshonda sighed, "I'll cover for you, but only if you come to the party tonight."

"Where is it anyway?"

"Slick Jimmy's place."

"Oh," Velvet drawled sarcastically. "Now I'm really tempted."

"Chill, girl," Malshonda said cheerfully. "Take away the baggy clothes and Slick Jimmy could be one *sexy-looking* dude. Believe me, big momma, *I* know sexy."

"Yeah," Velvet said drily. "Two legs and a dick, you'll find *anything* sexy."

"That's rude, girl."

"No, it's truthful."

"He could turn out to be a big star, and I could be *Mrs. Slick Jimmy*," Malshonda said. Then, lowering her voice, she added, "I didn't tell you this, but he's been dogging me for my number. The dude is ready to rock, and so am I."

"Get real, Malshonda. He's coming onto every girl on the set."

"Maybe," Malshonda said, unfazed. "Only those skanks ain't *me*. When it comes to guys, I got a little something, something that gets their blood boiling and their engine racing."

"Sure, you do. It's called a pussy."

"That's right!" Malshonda said, laughing. "And if I have anything to do with it, tonight it's gonna be a *working pussy*!"

Velvet loved her cousin, but the two of them were on

such different tracks. To Malshonda, it was all about getting laid and partying. To Velvet, it was allowing her talent to shine and working hard on her music. The last thing she needed was to be partying at Slick Jimmy's.

Later, she cornered Chanel. "Did you mean it when you mentioned you could get me in to see a modeling agent?"

"I certainly did," Chanel said, packing her brushes and make-up equipment into a large Fendi carry-all bag. "Why? You taking me up on it?"

"I'd like to," Velvet said hesitantly. "I mean, if you reallythink I've got what it takes."

"Don't be screwing with me," Chanel warned. "If I starthooking you up, you gotta be serious."

"I am," Velvet assured her.

"Then let's do it. I'll call a friend of mine and set something up."

"Honestly?"

"Done deal, babe. They're gonna love you."

Any excuse and Aretha took to her kitchen, cooking up a storm to celebrate her daughter's appearance in a video shoot. She was busy preparing fried chicken, sweet potatoes, monkey bread, hot rolls, cookies, and cakes.

Earlier, Malshonda had called to inform her that Velvet was also in the video. Aretha had immediately invited Fatima to join them.

When the girls arrived, the table was groaning withAretha's culinary delights.

Velvet was tired, her arm hurt and so did her ankle. All she *really* wanted to do was go home and start concentrating on her meeting with Tristin. What should she wear? How should she act? And, even more important, would he like her music?

Then her mother walked out of the kitchen, and she was

furious. She'd *told* Malshonda she didn't want to see her. The problem with Malshonda was that she never *listened.* As long as the prospect of getting laid was on her mind, she was unable to concentrate.

"So, girls," Fatima said, "I want to hear all about this video shoot. It sounds exciting."

Malshonda started filling her in, while Velvet retreated to the kitchen and helped Aretha place crispy pieces of fried chicken on a large platter.

"Put the dish in the center of the table," Aretha instructed her when they had finished. "Then get everyone to sit down. It's time to eat."

"Anyone else coming?" Velvet asked. "You've made enough food for the whole neighborhood."

"Only us, sweet girl," Aretha said, chuckling. "It's familynight. You and Malshonda can take food home for tomorrow. I know you girls never got nothing to eat at your place."

"We do," Velvet objected.

"No, honey, you don't, but that's fine as long as I feed you plenty here."

"You certainly do that."

"I understand you and your mama had a little talk," Aretha said, pausing to give Velvet a long and penetrating look.

"Who told you? Malshonda?"

"No, for once it wasn't my Malshonda. It was yourmama herself."

"And you believe everything she said?"

"Bout what?"

"Germany, and my daddy being dead and there's no way I can contact his family."

"If that's what she says, sweet thing," Aretha answered gently. "She'd have no reason to lie about something so important, now, would she?"

"I guess not."

"You know, your mama feels *really* bad, so maybe you should tell her that everything is all right between the two of you."

But it's not! Velvet wanted to scream. *It's not alright at all. I want a father just like everyone else.* "Sure," she said listlessly.

Aretha gave her a great big hug. "That's my girl. That's my little Vel Vel."

Von Diesel

Chapter Twelve

As she sat in Megan's hospital room, holding her friend's hand, Shemika tried to put everything in perspective. She was well aware that she'd made a mistake, a huge mistake. She'd had a one-night fling with a stranger who'd turned out to be not such a stranger afterall.

Touch's brother. His younger *half*-brother, who, from what she'd gleaned listening to the conversation at the table, had been living in Italy for the past three years. With Kareema, the gorgeous woman who had every man at the party completely entranced. And, extra bonus, he was an ex-druggie.

Yippee! How much better could it get?

"*Fuck!*" Shemika muttered, under her breath. She didn't usually swear, but this seemed like the perfect occasion todo so.

"What's the matter?" mumbled Megan, who for the past twenty minutes had seemed quite calm and peaceful. In the car, on their way to the hospital, she had spent twenty minutes howling frantically. Once they made it to the hospital in the waiting hall, she'd yelled, "GET ME MY FUCKING EPIDURAL!" at full volume, and kicked Tyrese in the balls.

Well, she'd had her epidural now and she was quite composed, lying there in a tranquil state.

A shaken Tyrese had gone to get coffee.

"I feel amazing!" Megan said dreamily. "Like I'm float-ing in the middle of the ocean on one of those rubber thingies."

"That's nice," Shemika said. "Drugs will do it every time."

"Sorry about your party."

"Don't be. It wasn't exactly going as I expected."

"Hmmm…" Megan murmured, not at all interested. "Baby out soon. Megan think again. New Jimmy Choos and Tiffany baubles. She closed her eyes, a smile hovering round her lips. "I feel so peaceful…"

Much as she wanted to, Shemika realized that this was neither the time nor the place to advise her best friend of the 'situation' she was caught in. Megan would probably listen without really hearing, smile and flip her the peace sign.

Megan's obstetrician had been and gone, promising to return shortly.

"I'm having a baby," Megan murmured, patting her over-extended stomach. "Isn't that something?"

"It sure is," Shemika agreed, squeezing her hand.

"A little Tyrese." Megan giggled.

"Not so little," Shemika corrected. "Your OB says this baby is going to be a big one."

"Tyrese will like that," Megan said, closing her eyes. "Tyrese will be *such* a proud papa…" And she drifted off into a happy half-sleep.

***

Two hours later, Tyrese junior was born, all eightpounds and six ounces of him.

The birth was effortless. A few pushes and the baby's curly black head entered the world. Shemika decided that whoever had invented epidurals was a major genius.

"Oh, my *God*!" Megan gasped, as a nurse wrapped the baby in a blanket and handed him to her. "This is a miracle!"

In the room for the entire delivery, Shemika and Tyrese had clutched each other in awe at how smoothly everything went.

"Congratulations," Shemika whispered to Tyrese. "And now it's time I left you three alone."

"Thanks for everything," Tyrese said, hugging her tightly. "I'm sorry you had to miss your party. We all are."

"Don't be silly. Seeing little Tyrese Junior enter the worldwas better than any party."

"Handsome little devil, isn't he?" Tyrese said, grinning proudly. "And well hung too!"

"Tyrese!"

"Just telling the truth."

"Anyway, he's fantastic!" Shemika raved. "He's got youreyes, and Megan's mouth."

"You're the best," Tyrese said, hugging her. "A truefriend."

She kissed Megan and the baby, then quietly made her way out. It was almost midnight and the maternity floor
was deserted. She hesitated a moment, then called Touch on her cell.

"Sweetheart!" he said, sounding more than pleased to hear from her. "I just got home this minute. Where are you?"

"Leaving the hospital now."

"Did everything go okay?"

"Yes. A healthy eight-pound six-ounce baby boy."

"I'll come get you and drive you to yourapartment."

"I can take a cab," she said, walking towards the elevator.

"Wouldn't hear of it. I'm on my way out of the door now."

"You don't have to."

"Yes. I do," he insisted. "You must be anxious to hear all about our party."

"I certainly am," she said. "Was my mother furious?"

"*You* know Nancy. But Kareema, Famous's girlfriend, saved the day. What a charmer! She had everyone under her spell, including Grandma Poppy. And, yes, *even* your mother."

"Great," Shemika said flatly, thinking this was *all* she needed to hear. Not only was Kareema the most beautiful girl she'd ever seen, apparently, she was the most charming too.

Ha! Lucky Famous.

Lucky Famous, the *seducer,* the *cheat,* the *ex-druggie* who got her drunk and lured her back to his apartment.

Screw *him*!

And yet…she'd gone willingly. She had not put up a fight. In fact, when he'd backed off due to her virginal state, *she* was the one who'd insisted he carry on.

He was *still* a cheat.

And what did that make her?

She didn't want to think about it. She didn't want to think about *him*. As far as she was concerned, it was one big nightmare she never planned on revisiting.

***

By the time Famous finally got Kareema out of the party, his Italian supermodel was *still* ready to rock 'n' roll.

"We go clubbing, *carino,*" she announced, throwing her arms round his neck and flicking her tongue across his lips. "Kareema felt like dancing."

Christ! She was the original Energizer Bunny. Wind her up and she'd go all night. When all he really wanted to do was clear his head and try to make sense of the night's events.

What the *fuck* was he going to do? Shemika Scott-Simon, the girl of his dreams, was about to marry his freaking bigshot brother, a man who could give her everything she wanted. Whereas he could give her, *what*? His undying love? It was wrong, all wrong, yet how could he stop it? What could *he* do?

Hang on. No need to get carried away. She was not the girl of his dreams: she was a one-night adventure, cheating on her fiancé. And yet she'd obviously never slept with Touch, so what was *that* about? How come she'd never had sex with her fiancé, but she was happy to jump into bed with *him*?

They needed to sit down and talk, discover the truth of the situation. And the sooner the better.

"*Carino!*" Kareema purred, her tongue snaking its way into his ear. "Where do we go now?"

Good question. Where *was* he supposed to take her?

He pulled out his cell and called Chanel. "I'm here with my girlfriend," he began, "and—"

"You found her!" Chanel exclaimed. "Who *is* she? What's the lucky girl's name? And even *more* important, is she as hot as you remember?"

"Uh…my *girlfriend*, Kareema, from Italy," he said pointedly, glancing at Kareema to see if she'd overheard.

"Oops!" Chanel exclaimed.

"She wants to go dancing," Famous continued. "Any ideas?"

"I'm on my way to meet Lenny D at Ralph and Kacoo's, then there's a party at Slick Jimmy's. You and your *girlfriend* can come with me."

"If you're sure…"

"Meet us at Ralph and Kacoo's, babe."

"You're the best, Chanel. We'll see you there."

***

Back at the hotel, Krush called Chi-rone for an update on his house.

"The news is not good," Chi-rone informed him. "They think your house was built on the site of an ancient landslide from the 1940's. Apparently all the builders wanted was the money. They didn't give a damn if at any time your crib would slip down the hill."

"Shit!"

"I'll contact the insurance agents first thing tomorrow. You're fully covered, right?"

"Who the fuck knows? Mudslides are a force of nature, don't think that's covered."

He hung up and couldn't sleep. Then he remembered the actress from the plane.Choosey Fallon. Talkative but still attractive, and tonight he definitely needed company.

She was staying in the same hotel, so even though it was almost midnight he took a chance, picked up the phone and called her. She answered on the second ring.

"I," he said."Who's this?"

"Krush Bentley. We sat next to each other on the plane."

"Of *course,* I remember," she purred. "What can I do for you, Krush?" *You can come to my room and suck my dick 'cause I'm too tense to sleep.*

"I'm sitting here on L.A. time unable to crash. I thought you might be doing the same."

"Actually," she confessed, "I'm watching a porno."

"You are?"

"Yes," she said, with a wicked laugh. "It's what I always do when I'm trapped in a hotel room by myself. *Very* relaxing. You should try it."

"Seems like a reasonable way to pass the time."

"I was thinking I could talk to Dave about it tomorrow on his show. Had to come up with *something* that'll outdo Drew and her tits."

"Sounds like a plan."

"It does, doesn't it?"

"How about coming down to my room and watching porn with me," said Krush."A three-second pause.

"Sure. Why not?"

Ten minutes later, they were making out on the couch. She wore a skimpy purple dress, short and low-cut. It did not take him long to maneuver her out of it. Underwear was not her thing. Neither was pubic hair. She was shaved to within an inch of her life and pierced right on her clit.

Naked, she straddled him. She had large erect nipples on small breasts. Real. Made a nice change.

She thrust them into his mouth, urging him to suck hard. He did so, and she shuddered to his touch. Within seconds, she was screaming like a wild woman. Then she bent her head to blow him, and he discovered that this was one trained actress. She had it down, the tongue-teasing and the hand-twisting. Stopping. Starting. Driving him fucking crazy.

When he came, there was an explosion big enough to make him forget about his house, Chilly, and Damiun.

He lay back on the couch and within minutes, had fallen into a much-needed deep sleep.

Von Diesel

Chapter Thirteen

Touch was waiting when Shemika walked out of the hospital. He jumped out of his car and grabbed her in a hug. "You're really a remarkable girl," he said, squeezing her tight.

"I'm not so remarkable," she said, extracting herself.

"Yes, you are," he insisted. "You stood up to your mother, you actually walked out on her. I don't care about you missing our rehearsal dinner because I didn't want it in the first place, but Carolyn was *not* happy."

"I'm sure she got over it after a while."

"She did," he said, holding open the car door for her.

"Good," she said, sliding into the passenger seat. "Thank God that I had Krush and Famous for support. I'm really getting to know the two of them. It's nice."

"Did they, uh, stay for the whole party?" she asked, thinking that, as far as she was concerned, it wasn't nice at all. In her eyes, Touch bonding with his brothers was a disaster.

"Let's just say they did their brotherly duty," Touch said. "And, as I told you on the phone, Kareema was charming everyone."

"Wonderful."

"You met Kareema, didn't you?""That Italian woman?"

"Yes. She's Famous's steady girlfriend. They livetogether in Italy. Apparently, she's a top model there."

"Nigel told me. She's doing the ad campaign for Ciccone.""What a striking girl," Touch said admiringly. "And a lot of fun."

"I'm sure she is," Shemika said, wishing he'd stop singing the woman's praises.

"Not as gorgeous as my Shemika, though," Touch said, reaching over to pat her on the knee.

"How long are they staying in New York?" Shemika asked, attempting to sound casual.

"Who?"

"Kareema and, uh…Famous." It was an effort to speak his name.

"I didn't ask," Touch said. "I'd like it if they could stay around for the wedding. Your mother would have to rearrange her seating, but I'm sure she can deal with that."

Oh yes, Famous at her wedding. How exciting was that?

She decided she had to do something special to makeit up to Touch. The guilt was killing her, especially now thatshe knew the identity of her mystery man.

"You need to get some sleep," Touch said, glancing at her. "What with the party and the upcoming wedding, you're under a tremendous strain."

"No, I'm not," she objected.

"You simply don't know it, sweetie."

"Touch," she said, putting her hand on his arm."Yes?"

"I'd like to go to *your* apartment."

"*My* apartment?" he said, surprised. "Why?"

"I was thinking that since I ran out on our party, it might be nice if we spent some quiet time together."

"It's late," he said, checking his watch.

"I know."

"And tomorrow's Monday."

"I know that too. But I still want to come to your apartment."

"Uh…Camryn and her nanny are staying the night."

"They'll be asleep, won't they?"

"Yes."

"Then it's okay if I come over."

"If that's what you want," he said reluctantly.

"Yes, Touch," she said softly. "That's exactly what I want."

***

"So," Kareema said, twirling her multiple bangles up and down her arm. "This friend of yours, what does she do?"

"Chanel is a top make-up artist," Famous said, hailing a cab. "You are gonna love her. Everyone does."

"You and this *friend*, you do the wild thing?"

"Babe!" he said, laughing. "No *way*. Chanel and I are purely platonic."

"Americans are so *timido* about sex," Kareema teased, getting in the cab.

"In Italy is *bene* to have sex with good friend. Nothing wrong, huh, *carino?*" "You're crazy," he said, jumping into the cab beside her.

"Where we meet your friend?"

"A drink at Ralph and Kacoo's, then she's taking us to a party. That's if you're not too beat."

"Me?" she said, laughing gaily. "Kareema *never* gets tired. Pour me champagne and I'm good as new."

***

Rushing into his apartment ahead of Shemika, Touch switched on lights and activated music.

"I'm not a guest, you know," Shemika said, following himin and smiling. "You don't have to entertain me."

"You very rarely come here," he said.

"That's because you never invite me."

"We are engaged, sweetheart. You'll be moving in here soon. Surely you know you're welcome at any time. I should give you a key."

They had decided that after the wedding, Shemika would move in with him until they found a new apartment. She could decorate any way she wanted.

She hadn't really given it much thought, getting married was scary enough.

"Can I get you a drink?" he asked.

"Orange juice. Is there a juicer in the kitchen?"

"I have no idea *what's* in the kitchen. My housekeeper takes care of that department."

"Let's go see."

His kitchen looked like it was never used. She found a juicer in one of the cabinets and some oranges in the fridge.

"Shall I squeeze you some too?" she asked, slicing the oranges in half.

"Do I look like I need a dose of vitamin C?" he said, amused.

"No, in fact I've been meaning to tell you how handsome you look tonight. I was proud to be at the party with you. Oh yes, and I *loved* our slide show. You were such a serious little boy. Do you realize you never smiled?"

"And *you* were unbearably cute."

"Unbearably?"

"I meant that as a compliment."

She handed him a glass of juice. "Drink up. It's good for you."

"*You*'re good for me," he said, coming up behind her and nuzzling her neck. "You really are, Shemika."

"I hope you understand why I had to leave the party tonight," she said quietly. "Megan needed me, and I promised her that when the time came I'd be there."

"It's admirable that you were there for your best friend."

They moved into the living room and sat down on the couch. Shemika snuggled up close and began to kiss him.

After a few moments he pulled away. "Shemika," he said warningly, "don't get me all hot and bothered, then go home."

"That wasn't my intention."

"Okay, *what*?" he said, bemused.

"Well," she said slowly. "We're getting married soon, and even though I told you I wanted to wait, I was thinking that tonight we should...do it."

"Now, hold on," he said, startled.

"Don't you want to?"

"Well, yes," he responded, although he wasn't at all sure that tonight was the night to sleep with his fiancée for the first time. Sadiya and her threats regarding Draygo were on his mind. Not to mention the upcoming face-to face with Red, followed by the crucial meeting with the Japanese bankers. And as if that wasn't enough, Camryn and Nanny Reece were sleeping in the guest room. Shemika's timing was totally off.

"Then...can I spend the night?" Shemika asked, unaware of what was going on in his mind.

"Are you *sure* about this?" he said, wondering how hecould talk her out of it.

"Absolutely."

***

There was the usual pushing and shoving crowd gathered outside Ralph and Kacoo's. Famous felt like a regular when the doorman waved him through as if he wasan old friend.

Hey, nobody was about to stop the fabulous Kareema. She blew the doorman a series of kisses, making the man's night.

They found Chanel and Lenny D ensconced at a corner table downing apple martinis. Chanel waved them over. "One drink, then let's go party!" she called out.

"*Ciao!*" Kareema said, dazzling everyone with her smile and flamboyant style.

"I'm a fan," Chanel said, acknowledging the Italian supermodel. "Seen you in all the Italian magazines."

"*Grazie*," Kareema said, loving any form of attention.

"And here's the news of the day," Chanel added. "I'm booked to do the make-up for your Ciccone shoot."

"*Bene!*" Kareema laughed. "This *piccolo* world, no?"

"Yeah," Chanel said,grinning. "V*ery* small."

"Famous, he do photos too," Kareema announced.

"You mean I finally get my hands on that face?" Chanelexclaimed.

"Is nice face," Kareema said affectionately, patting his cheek. "*Bello, si?*"

Lenny D was his usual non-talkative self, but Kareema quickly found out what he did and plied him with questions about his music. He soon livened up; she had that effect on men.

After twenty minutes Chanel suggested it was time to make a move.

"You *sure* you wanna go?" Famous asked Kareema, hoping she would flake out so they could go home, and he could let his mind run riot about Shemika, and what hewas going to do regarding their totally fucked-up situation.

"We go," she said, laughing that he should think otherwise. She winked at Chanel. "These boys, they have, how you say? no *energia*. You and I like to party, *si?*"

"You bet your ass," Chanel agreed, smiling broadly.

***

Now that they were alone in Touch's bedroom, it was awkward. They stood at the end of his oversize masculine-style bed, all dark wood and chocolate brown sheets. They'd been kissing for a while, but he didn't seem in any hurry to take it further.

Shemika realized she needed something to loosen up, she was treading on uncharted territory and it was making her nervous. Sleeping with Famous had been so spontaneous and unplanned, they'd fallen into bed together, filled with desire and passion. It had been a lustful, crazy, and most of all, insanely pleasurable experience.

Tonight, with Touch was different. First, she was stone-cold sober. Second, Touch wasn't making much of a move. *She* was the one kissing him, and although he was responding, he was allowing *her* to set the pace. Also, he wasn't the greatest kisser in the world.

"I think I'd like a drink," she said, in a small voice.

"What kind of drink?" he asked, drawing away from her.

"Vodka," she said tentatively.

"Sweetie, you *never* drink hard liquor."

"I'll make an exception."

"Look," he said, "if this is making you uncomfortable—"

"No, Touch," she said vehemently. "I *want* us to be together."

"So do I, sweetie, but tonight might not be the right time."

"The thing is, I need to relax," she said, ignoring him. "And a drink will do it. I missed out on the champagne at our party, so one little vodka won't hurt."

"Shemika," he said seriously, "you are stressed out. And,

much as I'd love you to spend the night, I think we should wait."

"You do?"

"We'll be married soon, so why rush into something you might regret?"

"But Touch—"

"No buts," he said resolutely. "Believe me, I *know* what's best for you."

How humiliating was this? Her husband-to-be had no desire to sleep with her. He was turning her down flat. Oh, *God!* She felt like such a fool.

"Get your coat, sweetie," he said, heading out of the bedroom. "I'm taking you home."

With that, he picked up his car keys from the hall table and started for the front door.

Chapter Fourteen

Party-time meant loud music, plenty of booze, writhing, sweaty bodies, and an over-abundance of weed so strong a person could get a contact high merely breathing the air.

This was all taking place in the living room of Slick Jimmy's basement house in Harlem, which he shared with two other rappers. The place was a comfortable dump with an insanely expensive sound system that was blasting hard-core rap.

Malshonda hit the scene and was in heaven. Velvet found a corner to lurk in, wishing she had not allowed Malshonda to talk her into coming. But that was their relationship, wasn't it? Malshonda was forever talking her into things she didn't want to do.

"You let that hoe walk all over you," Kev often complained. "Why don't you dump her and move in with me? You don't need her."

"Malshonda's like my *sister*, Kev, so don't be calling her a "hoe."

"She uses you 'cause you're so fine and she's so *not* fine."

"That's not a very nice way to talk. Malshonda would do anything for me."

Although sometimes she wasn't so sure. Malshonda *did* have a pushy way about her, and tonight was a prime example. Here she was, at a party she didn't want to be at, sitting in a corner by herself, while Malshonda was out there in the midst of it, coming onto every guy she could get her hands on.

But then again, Malshonda and her mom had taken her in when Fatima had pushed her out. She lived with them as though she *was* Malshonda's sister, and when it was time to move out, she and Malshonda had done it together. It was Malshonda who'd found them an apartment and scored them jobs at the coffee shop. Malshonda had *always* watched out for her, and yeah, maybe her cousin did use her sometimes because she was better-looking, but so what? Looks aren't everything, and Malshonda had a great big heart.

Since she didn't know anyone at the party, Velvet found herself stuck in the corner sorting through the many CDs stacked next to the sound system.

"Finding anything you like?" asked a familiar voice.

She turned around. It was Wahlee. "Oh, hi," she said, pleased to see someone she knew.

"You did great today," Wahlee said. "You could make yourself a living appearing in videos. You got the look."

"I have no plans to be 'The Girl' in the video," she said, half smiling. "I'm a singer-songwriter, didn't I tell you?"

"Maybe you did and maybe you didn't," Wahlee said, swigging from a bottle of beer. "But in *my* experience, you gotta use what you got. I wanted to be a dancer and look what happened to me."

"Directing's way cool."

"I enjoy it, and so does my wife. You should meet her,she's smart, like you."

"You're married?" Velvet asked, pleased that Wahleeconsidered her smart.

"Surprised?"

"You're young to be married."

Wahlee shrugged. "Twenty-eight. Got married 'cause my wife was knocked up and I didn't want to bring another child into the world who wasn't sure who her daddy was."

"That's cool," Velvet said. "What does your wife do?"

"She's a dancer," he said proudly. "Was she at the shoot today?"

"No, honey, not *that* kinda dancer. My wife's a ballet dancer."

"Wow! That's impressive."

"Yeah, she's one talented woman he said, taking another swig of beer. "You're bi-racial, right?"

"I'm not sure *what* I am," Velvet said, shrugging. "My mom's always telling me I'm black, but I have a feeling there's some white blood running through my veins."

"You don't know who your father is? Is that where this conversation's heading?"

"I never got to meet him. He died before I was born."

"Must've been tough for you," Wahlee said sympathetically.

"My mom raised me. She was a singer, but she gave it up."

"To do what?"

"It doesn't matter."

"Something bad, you can 't tell me?"

"Something dumb, I don't *want* to tell you."

"Here comes my wife," Wahlee said, as a brittle-looking white woman at least ten years older than him approached. Her dark hair was scraped back into a tight bun and she wore a long white dress. She did not seem particularly friendly as she gave Velvet a cursory nod, took Wahlee's arm and said, "You need to come with me." She promptly dragged him away.

So much for new friendships.

Malshonda was out on the dance-floor rocking and rolling with Slick Jimmy. Large as she was, she had plenty of rhythm and an abundance of style, Malshonda could shake it with the best of them.

Velvet wondered how long she'd have to stay at the party before she could leave, grab a cab, and go home. Malshonda wouldn't even notice she'd left.

So why was she waiting? Who did she think was going to appear?

Tristin?

Yeah, sure.

She looked around the room and thought, *Why would Tristin choose to hang out with these people?* They were just a bunch of stoners and Tristin didn't fit in. Although since Wahlee was here, maybe Tristin would come.

She wished Kev was with her. There was something soul-destroying about being at a party by yourself. It looked like you were trying to hook up or get laid, and she wasn't into doing either of those things.

Very slowly, she began edging towards the door.

And then it happened. Just as she was almost there, Tristin appeared.

As usual, he was Mr. Cool. Tonight, he was all in black, a giant Bentley cross hanging round his neck, Bentley studs in both ears, a circular watch, studded with Bentleys, and a short fur coat flung casually around his shoulders.

He gave her a quick glance, not at all surprised to see her. "Hey, Velvet," he said, flashing a friendly smile. "I got a new name for you."

"You do?" she said, determined to remain calm.

"Yeah, from now on I'm calling you Ms. V."

"Ms. V?" she questioned.

"Ms. Velvet," he said, with a lazy grin. "You dig?"

"If you say so."

"You're not leaving?"

"Uh…yes," she managed. "I kinda am."

"Got a ride?"

"Oh, sure," she murmured, recovering her composure. "I never go anywhere without my car and driver. He even drops me off at the coffee shop every morning."

"Funny girl."

"You think?"

They exchanged a long look.

"I gotta go say hello to Slick Jimmy, maybe hang for ten minutes," Tristin said. "If you wanna wait around, I'll drop you somewhere."

"That's okay," she said, feeling his heat.

"You don't wanna ride with me?" he said, pinning her with his sexy eyes.

"I didn't say that," she said, trying to control the dizzying effect he had on her.

"So chill," he said. "I'll go say hi to Jimmy, then we'll split."

"Okay," she found herself saying.

"You hungry?"

"I ate at my aunt's place. She's kind of a major cook."

"What'd she make?" he asked, moving closer, enabling her to get a whiff of his expensive cologne.

"Um, let me see. Tonight, she made fried chicken, honey spareribs and monkey bread. Lots of good things."

"Sounds like I need an invite."

"I don't think hanging at Aunt Aretha's is exactly your scene."

"Why not? Restaurant food gets tired, baby. There are times I *crave* a little down-home cooking."

"You do?" she said, wondering if his wife ever hustled her expensive ass into the kitchen. Probably not.

"Hey," he said, zeroing in with those eyes of his, "I'm a normal man with normal appetites."

"I'll see what I can arrange," she said, thinking there was nothing normal about Tristin Juzang. Then she started imagining Aunt Aretha's face if she ever got a close-up look at Tristin's outrageous bling. She'd crap herself!

Casually, he took her hand and led her over to Slick Jimmy, who was busy doing his thing with Malshonda. The two of them were not so much dancing, more like a whole lot of shaking and touching. Suddenly, Velvet realized she felt very comfortable with Tristin. They were totally in sync.

"Hey, it's my *man*!" Slick Jimmy yelled, stopping everything. The two men banged fists, followed by a macho hug.

Malshonda shot Velvet a *what-is-going-on-here?* look, while Velvet attempted to stay casual. Tristin let goof her hand and went over to greet Wahlee. Velvet noticed that Wahlee's wife cheered up at the sight of Tristin, the woman actually managed a tight-assed smile. After a few minutes of standing there, Velvet made her way back to her corner. She didn't think it was cool to be trailing around behind Tristin looking like she was some girl he'd picked up and was about to take home to screw.

The music was getting louder, the air was getting smokier, and she wondered how long it would be before Tristin chose to leave. She decided to give him ten minutes and then, ride or no ride, she was out of there.

Twenty minutes later, Chanel burst in with a group of friends. "This looks like a *party*!" she exclaimed, swooping down on Velvet. "You remember Famous, and this is *my* man, Lenny D."

Kareema grabbed Famous's arm. "Come, *carino*, we dance," she said, dragging him off into the moving throng.

"You here with Malshonda?" Chanel yelled, over the loud music.

"I was," Velvet shouted back. "She's over there with Slick Jimmy. They seem to have a thing going. I'm leaving soon."

"You need a cab?"

"Tristin's giving me a ride."

Chanel raised a disapproving eyebrow. "Tristin?"

"He's just dropping me off."

"Don't be forgetting what I told you," Chanel admonished. "Believe me, I'm not interested in seeing your sorry ass when he sweet-talks you into bed, and that's it. Tristin's never gonna change, you'd best remember that."

"He's not sweet-talking me into anything," Velvet said, annoyed that Chanel considered her such an easy mark.

"Hey, you've been warned. The man is a *player*, girl, so stay smart."

"Thanks for the advice, but I *do* know what I'm doing."

By the time Tristin was ready to leave, another half-hour had passed. Like a fool, Velvet had waited. Mad at herself, yet unable to resist, she had watched him from afar until he eventually came over, grabbed her hand, and led her outside to where his silver Cadillac Escalade with special wheel rims was parked curbside. He had a female uniformed driver standing to attention next to it.

"Get in the back, baby," Tristin ordered.

"Shouldn't I give the driver my address?"

"Thought we'd hit a coupla clubs," he said, leaning against the side of the car chewing on a toothpick.

"I don't feel like doing that."

"Then we'll stop by a bar, have ourselves a drink, get to know each other."

"I'm really tired," she said, trying not to sound pissed off, although she was madder at herself for hanging around waiting for him like some dumb groupie. "You took forever," she couldn't help adding.

"Yeah?" he said unconcernedly.

"Yes," she answered, realizing she probably sounded like

a nagging wife. Too bad. She wasn't about to jump.

"So, you're saying you don't wanna have a drink with me?" he asked, throwing her a quizzical look. "I'm getting a no, right?"

"It was a long day," she said, determined not to back down. "I'm ready to go home."

"If that's how you wanna play it."

"I'm not *playing* anything," she said, tossing back her long hair.

"No problem. Give my driver your address and she'll *take* you home."

"Aren't you coming?" she asked, surprised.

"No. The car will come back for me. I'm gonna party some more."

"You are?" she said, strangely disappointed.

"Got nothing else to do," he said, giving her a quick kiss on the cheek.

"See you tomorrow, Ms. V, six-thirty. Don't be late."

"I, I won't."

He started to walk away, then suddenly stopped and fixed her with another look. "You *sure* you don't wanna change your mind?"

"Positive," she said, although she wasn't positive at all.

Oh, God, if only he wasn't married...

"Got it," he said, Bentley's flashing. "See ya."

And with that he walked back into the house, and she was left by herself with nothing to do except wonder if she'd made the right decision.

Chapter Fifteen

Isha Parker studied the gold Rolex she'd stolen from Krush Bentley.

Usually, when she acquired a new piece of jewelry she sold it to her friendly neighborhood fence, but there was something about the gold Rolex she coveted. It was masculine and heavy, which made her wrist appear delicate and girlish.

She was standing in the bathroom of Red Bentley's apartment on 59th Street. Red Bentley, the billionaire. He was so old it was a shock that he could still get it up.

Her girlfriend and sometime partner in sex shows, Inka, had called her over on Saturday night, telling her there was money flying. Now it was late Sunday, and the old man was *still* going strong. Viagra. What a drug! It made worn-out old cocks strong again.

Isha sighed and felt sorry for all the tired old wives who were suddenly forced to deal with their husband's raging libidos.

She sucked in her cheeks as she admired herself in the bathroom mirror. Little Isha Parker from Slovakia.

Somebody should write a poem about her. She'd done well for herself. A tall, skinny, stick at school, the boys had taunted her, and the girls had avoided her because of her impoverished background. She'd compensated by giving the boys what they wanted, the kind of things they couldn't get from so-called nice girls. The result was that the boys chased after her, and the girls avoided her even more.

At sixteen, she'd run away from home and taken a train to Prague with her cousin Igor, and a car salesman who was twenty years her senior. The car salesman had introduced her to other men, and soon she was making money. After a while, she'd hooked up with an older girl from the Ukraine, Inka, who, at nineteen, had seemed very worldly. They hit it off and began putting on girl-on-girl shows, which were a big success until Inka took off for America with a rich businessman.

Two years later, Inka sent for her. She went willingly, paying for Igor to come too.

Inka had solid connections to whom she introduced Isha, and it wasn't long before they were known around New York as an extremely versatile and obliging team.

Now, three years later, Isha lived in a nice apartment. She had furs and jewels and made plenty of money. She had her own connections, and when anyone required a special girl in New York, she was top of the recommended list. Which was how she'd come to do the job for Patrick Sumter. It was a simple job, all she'd had to do was fuck the man Patrick told her to, and pass on a message. She'd been unable to resist adding her own PS to the message she'd left scrawled on his bathroom mirror. Actually, the guy was very attractive *and* excellent in the sack. But Isha had a rule, she never told men they were accomplished in bed, better to let them worry.

Inka started knocking on the bathroom door. "He wants you," Inka called out. "Hurry!"

Of course, he wants me, Isha thought, still admiring herself in the mirror. *I am the best.*

She strolled back into the bedroom, naked except for five-inch hooker heels and a low-slung belt of rhinestones around her waist, her flame-colored hair reaching below her waist, matching her pubic hair, dyed and groomed into a neat landing strip.

Inka had tied up the old man at his request. He was naked and decrepit, yet still unbelievably horny.

It occurred to Isha that he'd taken too many of those stupid blue pills. He could suffer a stroke or a heart-attack, and if he did, she was out of there.

The old man didn't look sick. He looked happy with a shit-eating grin on his leathery face. "Come on, girlies," he said encouragingly. "Let's see what you can do."

"Oh, *I* can do anything you want," Isha boasted, standing with her legs astride, hands on her hips. "*Anything.*"

***

Krush was woken at three a.m. by the phone. He'd forgotten to leave a "Do Not Disturb" on his line, which really pissed him off.

Choosey was long gone. Once the sex was over, so was she. "A girl has to get her beauty sleep," she'd said, quite coyly for a girl who, a few minutes earlier, had been screaming like a banshee. Then she'd left his suite, which pleased him because he hated it when he had to persuade bitches to leave.

It was Patrick on the phone.

"Been thinking about your idea," Patrick said, in his raspy voice. "I talked to my PR like you suggested, and since I ain't got my fucking money yet, we may as well make the most of this opportunity. We're gonna throw the fucking wedding for Chilly Rose."

"You got any idea what time it is?" Krush mumbled, staring in disbelief at the illuminated clock-radio by the bed.

"Who gives a fuck? You're lucky I'm talking to you."

"Yeah, lucky me," he said, covering a yawn.

"Lucky you are right," Patrick growled. "This doesn't mean you're off the hook with your debt. It buys you more time, that's the deal."

"Okay," Krush said, still half asleep. "Have your PR call me tomorrow. Chilly expects it to be special, and the media has to be strictly controlled."

"Thought I'd give you the word before you went running to Peter Morton."

"Yeah, yeah," Krush said, and slammed down the phone.

After that, he couldn't get back to sleep.

Should he call Choosey? No. Even she wouldn't come back at three a.m. Or maybe she would.

Then he started thinking. Why was sex so important in his life? Why had he always depended on it?

He knew why. Sex was his sleeping pill, his comfort zone. Famous had chosen drugs and booze, Touch had thrown himself into work while *his* vice was sex. Although, gambling had recently come a close second.

After a while, he got out of bed and began pacing around the suite, finally settling in front of one of the huge windows. He gazed out at the view, admiring the city. New York was so beautiful at night. The sparkling lights and the streams of traffic looking like toys as they negotiated their way up and down the narrow streets.

Before long, his mind was buzzing. Tomorrow, breakfast with Famous, then the meeting with Red, and after that he'd get on a plane and fly home.

Yeah, fly home. To *what?* No house, that was for sure.

How depressing was *that?*

He'd lost everything, and the kicker was he couldn't even afford to rebuild until Patrick was paid off.

No more gambling. The call of the tables had lost its lure.

***

It was almost four a.m. by the time Famous finally persuaded Kareema to leave the party.

"I *love* New York," Kareema cried, throwing herself intoa cab, bracelets jangling. "We spend more time here, *si*?"

"Yeah, New York's great," Famous agreed, yawning. "Especially when a person can get some sleep. Don't you have to work tomorrow?"

"Not until the afternoon. *We* go for fittings, you come too."

"Can't wait!" he said, yawning again.

"Is *bene, carino*. They insist big name, but I say no, *you*."

"I'm big in Italy," he pointed out.

"Italy one thing, America another," Kareema said sagely. "The ad campaign will be in all magazines. Is good for you, *si*?"

"It can't hurt."

"This Slick Jimmy," Kareema mused. "I like his music. It's a heavy beat, but good, huh?"

Everything was good, as far as Kareema was concerned. She was getting on his nerves. All he wantedto do was crawl into bed and get some sleep. Then he realized he'd only manage a few hours because he'd promised Krush he would join him for breakfast.

Kareema's hand began moving up his thigh. Christ! The woman was insatiable.

He removed her hand. His energy was spent. Mentally and physically, he needed time out.

"Something the matter, *carino*?" she asked, lookinghurt.

"If I told you," he said wearily. "You'd never under-stand."

***

Lady J Bentley did not sleep, she was too disturbedeven to contemplate closing her eyes. She stayed up, waiting for Red to come home, determined to confront him.

Sometime in the early hours she realized he was staying out all night again.

She suspected he was *still* cavorting with whores.

To think she'd wasted six years with a despicable human being, a selfish billionaire incapable of loving anyone except himself. It was a travesty.

And the truth was that he probably did *not* love himself.

How could he when his lifelong focus had always been ruining other people's lives?

Chapter Sixteen

"You're like a guy," Famous complained, as Kareema straddled him before he even had a chance to open hiseyes.

It was Monday morning and he had, like, three hours sleep and now his so-called girlfriend was taking advantage of his piss hard-on and crawling all over him.

Kareema was perpetually horny. Sleep, no sleep, shewas always in the mood.

At least he didn't have a hangover. Back in the day he would've been wrecked, incapable of speech, unable to move. His head would've been pounding, his body quivering with misuse. Now he was merely tired.

Kareema, who'd spent the night imbibing everything from margaritas to champagne, seemed to be suffering noill-effects. She was chirpy and horny, even her breath wassweet.

"What the fuck?" Famous groaned. "Can't you wait until I hit the john?"

"Why waste a good thing, *carino?*" Kareema replied, lowering herself onto him, so that he slid inside her with no chance of escape.

Once he was on board, nature took its course, and before long he was as into it as she was. They rode the wave for at least ten minutes, both adept at holding back. When it was time, they came together in perfect unison.

"*Fantastico!*" Kareema exclaimed. 'my Yankee boyfriend is *buono!*"

"Don't *say* that."

"*Scusa?*"

"Yankee boyfriend", it sounds dumb."

Kareema shrugged and got out of bed. "I take shower," she announced, stretching like a cat.

"Do you mind if I take one first?" he said quickly. "Gotta

meet my brother for breakfast."

"We shower together," Kareema decided, striding toward the bathroom.

"*Bene, carino?*"

Oh yeah, sure, *bene*. Given half a chance, this woman would be quite happy to fuck him to death.

***

Once more Krush was awoken by the phone. This time it was morning, and on the line was a tearful Chilly Rose, informing him that she was finished with Brewsky, and he should immediately cancel their Las Vegas wedding.

This woke him up with a vengeance. Cancel the freaking wedding just when he'd got Patrick Sumter all fired up about having it at his hotel? No way. "What's the problem?" he asked.

"You were right about Brewsky," Chilly sobbed. "He's a pig."

"I never said he was a pig," Krush said patiently. "I merely said you should be sure you're making the right decision."

"Well, I am," Chilly said, sounding like a truculent little girl. "I'm making the decision to, like, *never* see him again!"

"What did he do?"

"I can't tell you," she wailed.

"You'd better," he responded, wondering how he was going to break the news to Patrick.

"Can't!"

Oh, shit. It was obviously something bad that she would expect him to take care of. "You can tell me, Chilly," he said, in a low, comforting voice. "You know you can tell me anything."

A long pause while she thought about it. "Okay," she said at last. "Only it's gotta stay between us, Krush. Promise?"

"What?" he coaxed.

"He called me ugly."

"*Ugly?*"

"Yes, ugly," she said indignantly. "Don't you *dare* laugh at me, Krush."

"Who's laughing?"

"He said I was a spoiled, ugly, little girl, and he was leaving. So then he, like, *left,* and I *never* wanna see him *again.*"

"Hmm…Well, you *know* you're not ugly. *People* magazine just picked you as one of their fifty most beautiful. You're on the cover of *W* and *Rolling Stone.* The guy is delusional if he called you ugly."

"I know. And I'm not even *pregnant* anymore."

At least there was *some* good news. "Ignore him," Krush said. "He's obviously a moron."

"You bet he *is,*" she said fiercely. "A big, *fat,* horny, moron."

"Do you want me to come over later?"

"Hang on," Chilly whispered excitedly. "I think he just walked in. I'll have to call you back."

So much for never wanting to see the big, fat, horny, moron again.

Krush got up and stretched. His body was screaming for a workout, and not the sexual kind. He decided to hit the gym and relieve some of the stress he knew was building up inside him.

***

Touch's housekeeper, Mrs. Conner, a middle-aged stout

woman, originally from Scotland, set a second batch of pancakes on Camryn's plate.

"Me *like* pancakes," Camryn said, licking maple syrup off her fingers.

"I know you do, dear," said Mrs. Conner.

"Me too," Touch agreed, glancing up from the *New York Times*. "You make 'em good, Mrs. Conner."

"Thank you, Mr. Bentley."

"Me *like* staying with my daddy," Camryn crooned, tilting her head to one side. "Daddy! Daddy! *My* daddy!"

"You're a lucky girl," Mrs. Conner said, giving Camryn a pat on the head.

"Lucky! Lucky! *Lucky!*" Camryn shrieked.

"When Daddy marries Shemika and we move into a new apartment," Touch said, lowering his newspaper, "we're going to decorate your room any way you like. What do you think of *that*?"

"Camryn *likes* Hello Kitty," Camryn crooned, clapping her hands together.

"Hello Kitty *bed*, and *sheets*, and *floor*, and *ceiling*, and all over my *face*." She burst into a fit of giggles. "All over Daddy's face too!"

"Thanks."

"And Daddy's *butt*!" she said, giggling even more.

"Excuse me?"

"Butt! Butt! *Butt!*"

"That's no way for a lady to speak," he said sternly.

"Camryn's not a *lady*, Daddy," she said, all wide-eyed and innocent. "Camryn's a little girl."

"Who taught you to say butt?"

"Don't say it again. Not nice."

Nanny Reece entered the breakfast room. "We should be on our way, Mr. Bentley," she said, stiff English accent firmly in place. "I have to get Camryn changed for school."

"My driver's downstairs," Touch said. "I'll come with you. I need to speak to Mrs. Bentley."

"Very well," Nanny Reece said. "Come along, Camryn."

"Come along, Camryn," the little girl mimicked. "Come along! Come along! *Come along!*"

She raced over to Mrs. Conner and gave her a big hug. "Camryn go school now. Bye."

"Be a good girl," Mrs. Conner said. "Don't be doing anything *I* wouldn't do."

Camryn giggled and dashed out of the room.

Touch put down his newspaper and stood up. He'd been scanning the paper, searching for any stories of unidentified murder victims. Now he thought how foolish he was to have believed Sadiya and her threats against Kashif. He told himself once again that she was lying as usual. Bluffing and lying, for that was her way.

Today, he planned on clearing things up. First on his agenda was setting Sadiya straight.

He was going to make *sure* that Kashif was deported. It was the only answer.

"Hi," Shemika said. "How do you *feel?*"

Megan was sitting in her hospital bed, propped up by several pillows. The baby was lying in a crib next to her.

"Like a truck zipped through my snatch," Megan said, making a face. "Other than that, I'm perfectly fine."

"Sounds painful."

"Is painful. Only every time I take a peek at Tyrese Junior, it's definitely worth it."

"He's so gorgeous," Shemika said, bending down and

peering into the crib. "Those eyelashes!"

"Never mind the eyelashes, how about his thingy?" Megan quipped. "It's all Tyrese can talk about. My husband is obsessed!"

"Typical," Shemika said, smiling. "The proud papa."

"Oh, he's proud all right. He cannot wait to tell anyone who'll listen that size runs in the family!"

"I think that's rather sweet."

"I'll let you know," Megan said, taking a sip of water. "You're here early. Everything okay?"

"I wanted to see you before I went to work."

"Because..."

"Because nothing. You just had a baby, so I thought you'd appreciate an early-morning visit."

"Sure," Megan said disbelievingly, moving around in search of a more comfortable position. "*You've* got something on your mind. You *know* you can never hide anything from me."

"Hmm..." Shemika murmured.

"Hmm *what?*"

"You *do* know me," Shemika said, perching on the edge of the bed.

"So?"

"Mystery Man."

"What about him?" Megan asked eagerly.

"He's not a mystery anymore."

"Oh, no! You *didn't*," Megan exclaimed. "You *bad* girl, you went to his apartment."

"Certainly not."

"What, then?"

"At the party last night, did you happen to notice Touch's brother, the young one?"

"The guy with the Italian model?"

"That's the one."

"What about him?"

"Uh...did he look familiar to you?"

"Now that you mention it..." Then Megan got it. "No!" she yelled, sitting up straight. "You are *kidding* me! That's *impossible!*"

"Unfortunately, it's true," Shemika said, feeling better for sharing. "Mystery Man is a mystery no more. Mystery Manis Famous Bentley, Touch's brother."

And before Megan could react further, Tyrese came bounding in laden with flowers, magazines, and a big boxof chocolates.

"Hi, girls," he said. "What's going on?"

***

Krush left a message at the desk for Famous to meet him at the hotel gym. He should've thought about working out before, he needed a boost of energy.

The first person he ran into at the gym was Choosey. She was jogging on one of the treadmills clad in shorts and a stomach-baring red tank. "Hi," she said, waving at him as if they were no more than casual acquaintances.

And actually, he thought, that was *all* they were–casual acquaintances who'd enjoyed a vigorous late-night fuck.

"Hey," he responded, making his way to the racks of weights.

There were a few other people in the gym, but no one he knew. He warmed up for a few minutes, then started lifting, enjoying the pull on his muscles, feeling the burst ofstrength that working out always gave him.

He couldn't help wondering that if Red hadn't summoned him to New York, would he still have lost hishouse? Had he stayed in L.A., was there *some* way he could've saved it?

Common sense told him no. Fantasy told him yes.

Damn Red Bentley. Anything he touched turned to shit.

He shouldn't have come running to New York. It had been a mistake. He didn't want the old man's money, afterall. It wasn't worth the price.

And there *would* be a price. Oh, yes, with Red Bentley there was *always* a price.

***

Famous did not believe in relationships. Relationships were crap. Strictly for people who wanted to spend the rest of their sorry lives tied to one person.

Then he'd met Shemika. Then he'd slept with Shemika.

And suddenly he was a believer.

Only one problem. Shemika, as it turned out, was his big brother's fiancée.

How lucky was *that*?

So, what the hell did she see in Touch?

Boring Touch, who put business before all else. Dull Touch, who only shone in the boardroom.

Uptight Touch, who, no doubt, was a total dud in bed.

Striding down Park Avenue on his way to meet Krush, he still couldn't get Shemika off his mind. The wedding was coming up, and he felt totally helpless because there was nothing that he could do to stop it. Absolutely nothing.

Unless of course…he told Touch the truth.

That was a thought. Tell big brother the truth and watch Shemika's world crumble.

No, he couldn't do that to her. She was too special. She deserved better than him opening his big mouth.

He had to see her, that was for sure. He was determined to find out what was on her mind when she'd come back to his apartment and slept with him.

But how was he going to arrange to meet her without Touch finding out?

Krush would have an answer. Krush was an expert at figuring things out.

***

Sitting in the back of Touch's car with Nanny Reece, Camryn chatted all the way to the apartment. She commented on everything as she gazed out of the window.

"Look, Daddy, see the big dog."

"Look, Daddy, funny man lying down on the sidewalk."

"Look, Daddy, see the horsey go poop!"

"Language!" Touch said, causing Camryn to dissolve into one of her giggling fits.

"Poop! Poop! *Poop!*" Camryn screamed, her face bright red with excitement. "Poop! Poopie! Poo*pie!*"

"That's enough," Touch said, turning round to glare at Nanny Reece, who sat there like a stoic lump. He decided it was time to have a word with Sadiya about her choice of nanny. This woman had zero personality, and no control over his child.

When they arrived at the building, Camryn jumped out of the car and raced inside. Nanny Reece followed at a snail's pace.

Touch glanced at his watch. It was just before eight. He had a little time before the nine o'clock meeting with Red.

"Wait here," he instructed his driver. "I'll be out in fifteen minutes."

Riding up in the elevator, Camryn started a tuneless rendition of "Itsy Bitsy Spider". "Do you *like* spiders, Daddy?" she inquired, stopping for a moment, all wide-eyed and cute.

"*I* don't, 'cause they go all crawly up your legs and into your *butt.*" More screams of laughter. "Butt! Butt! *Butt!*"

Nanny Reece didn't say a word. Touch was developing a major headache.

Spending time with his daughter could be quite exhausting. The elevator ground to a stop, and all three of them got out.

Touch realized he should probably have called first. He hated it when Sadiya greeted him in one of her floating negligees, her breasts barely contained by the flimsy material. It had happened a few times, and he was certain she was hoping he'd get turned on. Actually, the opposite happened. He got completely turned off.

Nanny Reece produced her key and opened the front door to the apartment.

Determined not to get involved in a fight, Touch knew exactly what he was going to say to his ex-wife, and this time she'd better start listening.

"Mommy!" Camryn yelled excitedly, racing across the marble foyer. "Mommy! Mommy! Mommy! Camryn's *home.*"

Touch headed for the living room. "Tell Mrs. Bentley that I'm here," he said to Nanny Reece. "And make sure she knows I'm in a hurry."

As he said "hurry", Camryn began to scream. They were piercing screams, and they were coming from Sadiya's bedroom.

"Christ!" he said irritably, as Camryn's screams attacked his almost formed headache. Turning to Nanny Reece, he said, "Don't you have *any* control over Camryn whatsoever?"

"Excuse *me*?" Nanny Reece said, her back stiffening.

"My *child* is screaming. *Do* something about it."

At that moment Camryn came racing back, her dress and hands covered with blood. "Mommy's sick!" she yelled hysterically. "My mommy's sick! Sick! *Sick!*"

Von Diesel

Chapter Seventeen

"Slick Jimmy's got moves I only ever dreamed about!" Malshonda raved, bursting into the apartment early on Monday morning, her face flushed with excitement. "He's hung like a freaking stallion, and that man knows how to go down and *then* some!"

"You didn't show up for work today," Velvet said accusingly. "You were supposed to be there at six this morning. Aaron called earlier. He was *really* pissed about neither of us coming in. I told him you had the flu. You know, Malshonda, you *promised* you'd cover for me. We really let him down."

"Who gives a shit?" Malshonda said. "We got loot now, we're moving up. No more working our asses off slinging hash and pouring coffee."

"Wrong," Velvet corrected, always the responsible one. "That money is to pay off our bills, remember? We still need to keep our jobs."

"Not *me*. Jimmy's scoring me a gig singing back-up on his tour."

"Are you serious?"

"Yup, this girl is *dead-on* serious. I'm moving out and going on the road. How ace is *that*?"

"For real?" Velvet said, shocked.

"For *damn* real. The dude is apeshit 'bout me, so I'm taking advantage of the situation."

"Malshonda, you don't know—"

"Oh, I *know*," Malshonda said confidently. "I know that I finally found me a man who's gonna give me everything I want."

"What about our apartment?" Velvet asked. "If you're splitting, where does that leave me?"

"I know it's sudden, little cous'," Malshonda said, sounding guilty, "but I was thinking you might wanna movein with Kev. He's always dogging you to do that, and the two of you make a hot couple."

"You really think I'd move in with Kev because that'll make it easier for you to dump on me?" Velvet said, tryingto control her growing irritation.

"I *ain't* dumping on you. All I'm doing is shaking things up, looking to my future."

"Great! And what am I supposed to do?"

"You're the smart one, you're gonna be fine."

"When are you leaving?"

"Jimmy's coming back for me in a coupla hours. I'm throwing some stuff in a bag, then I'm outta here."

"So that's it, you're going today?"

"Hey, the man wants to keep me close. I ain't arguing with *that*."

"This is crazy. You hardly know him."

"Ooh, I know him *good*," Malshonda said, hurrying into the bedroom. "That fool is one hot boy, and I ain't letting him outta my sight."

"Then I guess this means you're giving up your job atthe coffee shop?" Velvet asked, following her.

"A girl's gotta do what a girl's gotta do," Malshonda said, tossing an assortment of clothes into a large duffelbag. "And this be my destiny."

"After one night it's your destiny," Velvet said, shaking her head in amazement. "Man, that's really something. Who's telling Aaron you're not coming back?"

"I was thinking you'd do it for me."

"Gee, thanks."

"Don't go getting down on me, Ms. V.," Malshonda said, making a face. "I know it's sudden and all, but I *gotta* do this, and *you* gotta understand."

"You're not giving me much choice."

"It's not *your* choice, girl, it's *mine*."

"If it's what you want…"

"It's *definitely* what I want. Only don't be telling my mom, she'll throw a shitfit."

Velvet nodded, trying to make sense of what was happening. Malshonda was making a move, and who knew if it was the right one? Since there was no stopping her, Velvet realized she'd better start thinking about herself.

Kev was due back at any minute. Not that she planned on moving in with him, Kev was a nice enough guy, but she wasn't looking for commitment.

Her immediate problem was what to do about the apartment. She'd have to look for somewhere smaller, either that or find a roommate to share the rent because there was no way she could afford it on her own.

Things were changing fast, but that was okay, she could handle it.

After loading two duffel bags with clothes, Malshonda finally shifted the attention off herself and asked Velvet what had happened between her and Tristin. "I *saw* you sneaking out with him last night," Malshonda said, wagging her finger. "You *know* we got a rule about married dudes."

"Then I guess you saw him sneaking back *into* the party, 'cause all he did was tell his driver to drop me home."

"You asking me to believe he didn't try to jump you?" Malshonda said, raising her eyebrows.

"He was a gentleman all the way."

"*Sheeit*! That's boring, girl."

"Not to me."

"The dude was playing it tight, all the better to worm his way into your panties."

Velvet shrugged, discussion over. She didn't want to share her feelings about Tristin with anyone, not even Malshonda. "How about I make us some eggs?" she suggested. "You must be hungry."

"Don't be all pissed at me," Malshonda wailed, putting on her please-forgive-me-cause-I'm-adorable voice. "You *know* how much I love you, little cuz."

"I'm not mad. I understand."

"I was thinking I'd give you all my money from the videoshoot. Add that to your money, and you'll be okay till you decide what you're gonna do."

Didn't Malshonda ever listen? The money from the video shoot was earmarked to pay off all their outstanding bills. "Stop worrying about it, Malshonda," she said.

"I'll manage."

"Maybe later I can get *you* a gig singing back-up with me."

"No, thanks," Velvet said, thinking there was nothing she'd like less. "Slick Jimmy's music isn't my style."

"Oh," Malshonda said, insulted. "I guess you'd soonerbe slinging hash and shoveling eggs?"

"I'm not doing *that* forever. Something will come along."

"Sure, it will," Malshonda said magnanimously. "You gotta have faith, girl. God will protect you. He always does."

Later, when Malshonda had finally left, the full realization of what had just taken place dawned on her. She was totally alone. No Malshonda to hang with, go shopping, share the cooking, read magazines, watch TV, catch the occasional movie, although they always argued about who was sexier, Denzel Washington or Blair Underwood. Velvet opted for Blair; he was one fine lookingspecimen who didn't work enough for her liking.

Of course, she'd still have Kev, but a boyfriend was a

whole different ball game. Boyfriends were good for sex and cuddling, killing bugs and fun. They came up short on real camaraderie. At least, that was her experience.

Kev called as soon as he got back into town. "How you feelin', sugar?" he asked, over the phone. "Cause I'm feeling *in* the mood."

"I'm better," she said.

"Then I'll come get you. We can grab a burger, a beer,and go back to my place."

Ah, yes, a burger and beer. Mr. Romance is back intown.

"Can't tonight," she said.

"How come?"

"Cause I promised Aaron I'd work the late shift, seeing as how I've been off," she lied. For some reason she didn't want to tell Kev about her upcoming meeting with Tristin.

"Sugar—" he began.

"Sorry, Kev. I know it's a drag."

"Wanna come by when you're through?"

"No."

"*No*, my girl says. That's a stunning welcome back."

"I'll be tired. Maybe tomorrow night."

"You got it."

"There's a new song I've been working on."

"Don't you *ever* take a rest?"

"I want you to hear it, see what you think."

"Tomorrow it is."

She didn't mean to deceive Kev, but her meeting with Tristin had nothing to do with him, and right now, just in case nothing came of it. She'd decided to keep it to herself.

Tristin Juzang. Even his name sent chills down her spine.

Von Diesel

Chapter Eighteen

"Your wife was stabbed six times," Detective Rodriguezsaid. "Six times," he repeated.

Slumped in a chair in the living room of Sadiya'sapartment, Touch stared at the man, his face full of disbelief.

"Do you have any idea who could've done this?"Detective Rodriguez asked, peering at him intently.

"I thought you said it was a robbery," Touch stated.

"I didn't say it *was*," Detective Rodriguez replied. "What I *did* say was that it *might* have been. Start listening to me, Mr. Bentley, it's important."

Touch was still in shock. The events of the morning were fresh in his mind as it had only happened less than half an hour earlier. After Camryn had emerged, screaming, he'd followed Nanny Reece into the bedroom where they'd discovered Sadiya sprawled across her bedin a pool of blood. The room had been ransacked.

Stoic English Nanny Reece had become hysterical.Touch had been forced to shake her. "For God's sake, you're supposed to be looking after Camryn," he'd shouted. "Pull yourself together and get her away fromhere. Take her to a neighbor, anywhere."

"But, Mr. Bentley, your wife is dead. She's *dead*."

"We don't know that," he'd said, although he knew she was, there was so much blood that Sadiya couldn't still be alive.

Christ! Where was Camryn? He'd run out of thebedroom to find her.

His little daughter was sitting on the floor in the hall, whimpering softly. "Everything's going to be all right, sweetheart," he'd said, sweeping her into his arms. "Nanny's taking you to some friends, and Daddy will comeget you in a little while. Mommy's not feeling very well."

"Okay, Daddy," Camryn said, tears rolling down her cheeks. "I be a good girl, Daddy. I be *very* good."

"Yes, sweetie, I know you will." He'd turned to Nanny Reece, who looked as if she was about to lose it again. "Are there any friends you can take her to in the building?"Nanny Reece nodded.

"Go and stay there until I come for her. Call down tothe desk clerk and tell him what apartment you'll be in."

"Yes, Mr. Bentley."

As soon as they were gone, he'd picked up the phone and dialed 911. "I'm reporting a–a murder," he'd stammered. "Or...a dead person. I–I'm not sure. My–my ex-wife, she's–she's lying on her bed–covered with blood."He'd given them the address, then taken up a position by the door.

Within five minutes, a patrol car arrived downstairs. A few minutes later, two policemen walked into the apartment.

"Is anyone else here?" one of the cops asked, looking around, his hand hovering near his gun.

"No, I, I just got here myself."

"Where's the body?"

"My daughter was with me, and her nanny…We walked in and found her."

"*Who* exactly did you find?"

"My ex-wife."

"Where is she?"

"In the bedroom," he said, indicating the way.

"Okay, sir. A detective will be here shortly," the cop assured him. "Do not touch anything. I suggest you go sit in the living room and wait."

So that was exactly what he'd done, too shocked to do anything else.

In the back of his mind, he knew he should call his lawyer. But why would he do that? He wasn't guilty of anything. Yet every time he saw a murder on TV or in a movie, the husband or ex-husband was always the mainsuspect.

Jesus! He wasn't thinking straight. It was ridiculous.

He'd walked into the apartment with Camryn and her nanny, there was no way anybody could possibly suspect him.

Besides, he *knew* who'd done it. Kashif. He had no doubt about *that*. Draygo Kashif had murdered Sadiya,because who knew what the two of them had going onbetween them?

Touch stared at the overweight Hispanic detective. The man had a small, annoying black moustache and crooked front teeth. He wore glasses and his jacket was too tight for his large frame.

"I *am* listening, Detective," he said, attempting to pull himself together. "This is a terrible shock."

"I understand, Mr. Bentley," Detective Rodriguez said, producing a well-used notebook and a stubby pencil. "But,as I'm sure you're aware, I do have to ask you some questions."

"I'll tell you what I can," Touch said, still trying to clear his head. "It won't be much,\ because Mrs. Bentley and Iare, *were*, divorced."

"Amicable?"

"Excuse me?" Touch said, hunching forward.

"Were the two of you fighting? Having any problems?"

"No."

"You're *sure* about that?"

"Yes, I'm sure."

"Hmm…" the detective said, scribbling something in his notebook.

"What does *that* mean?" Touch said, taking offence atthe detective's attitude.

"Did the *ex*-Mrs. Bentley have any enemies?" Detective

Rodriguez asked, still scribbling.

"I shouldn't think so."

"Was she seeing anyone?"

"Why are you asking *me*?"

"I thought you might know."

"Well, I *don't*."

"Where were *you* last night, Mr. Bentley?"

"Excuse me?"

"Where *were* you last night?" Detective Rodriguez repeated.

"I was at a party. My rehearsal dinner actually."

"Rehearsing for *what?*"

"It was my rehearsal dinner," Touch said, speakingslowly. "I'm getting remarried."

"Really?" Detective Rodriguez said, scribbling furiously. "And I guess your ex wasn't too happy about *that*."

"What does my getting married again have to do with anything?"

"You never know," Detective Rodriguez said mysteriously. "Now, tell me, Mr. Bentley, what time exactlydid you leave this…rehearsal dinner?"

Touch frowned. He didn't like the way things weregoing. "Do I need to call my attorney, Detective?" he asked.

"I don't know," Detective Rodriguez replied, giving him along penetrating look. "Do you?"

***

"Come with me while I run upstairs and take a quick shower," Krush said, as they left the hotel gym. "Then we'd better get going. Don't want to be late for Daddy, oh."

"Wish you'd told me that you were working out," Famousremarked, as they headed for the elevator. "I could've joined you instead of standing around watching."

"Why didn't you?"

"I'm not exactly in workout clothes."

"You could've borrowed something," Krush pointed out. "I'm sure they have stuff here."

"Nah, it was more fun watching you," Famous said, not even bothering to eyeball the pretty blonde getting out of the elevator as they got in. "You're kinda buff for a lawyer. How come?"

"I used to have my own gym, that was before my house got mud-slimed."

"I meant to ask, what're you doing about that?"

"I'll figure things out when I get back to L.A. I'm not even sure what the insurance covers if anything."

"Man, it's a real bummer," Famous commiserated. "Don't worry about me, you've got enough on your mind."

"I'd sooner you didn't remind me," Famous said, grimacing.

"You can't hide from it," Krush pointed out. "You have to decide how you're going to handle the situation."

"You're right," Famous said glumly. "I can't pretend it never happened, and Shemika can't pretend I don't exist."

"Have you thought about how you're going to contact her?"

"I'll come up with something."

Easy to say, but what exactly was he going to come up with? He felt so damn helpless.

Krush's cell rang. It was Chilly, informing him in an excited whisper that all was cool, and the wedding was back on.

Big surprise.

They reached his suite where a maid was already cleaning the bathroom. "Five minutes," Krush said, slipping her a twenty-dollar bill, "and we'll be out of here."

He showered quickly, dressed, and met Famous in the living room. "I'm not sure if I can stomach seeing the old bastard today," he said, downing a glass of orange juice from the room-service trolley. "What's he going to tell us? That he's not leaving us one dime, that he doesn't *have* to?"

"Hey, he's gotta leave his money to *somebody*." Famous pointed out, biting into an apple. "He's a freaking*billionaire*. He's too cheap to leave it to charity, and we allknow he hates everyone else."

"He hates us too," Krush stated.

"What makes you think it's about money anyway?" Famous asked. "It could be—"

"Could be *what*?" Krush interrupted. "In Red's warped mind money is the only hold he still has over us. And you know what? I'd rather be broke than beg anything from him."

***

"You're here early," Nigel said, greeting Shemika at the office. "Your mother's been on the phone already. I should warn you; she sounds as if she's on the warpath."

"Not again!" Shemika sighed.

"Yes, again," Nigel said crisply. "Where were you? According to her, she called your apartment three times this morning and got no answer."

"I stopped by the hospital to see Megan."

"How *is* the darling girl?"

"She's doing great, the baby is beyond gorgeous, and Tyreseis ecstatic."

"I presume that last night you got to the hospital in time."

"Just about."

"Thank God! I had visions of you delivering Megan's babyin the back of Touch's car!"

"It didn't happen," she said, smiling.

"Well, all I can say is you missed *some* night," Nigel announced.

"I heard. Touch picked me up from the hospital."

"Naturally, Marcello ruined the *entire* evening for me," Nigel complained, narrowing his eyes. "He's *such* a slut."

"What did he do this time?"

"Flirted with Sassy's toy-boy all night. As you can imagine, I was *livid*!"

"I think you've got to face up to the fact that you're reaching the end of your relationship," Shemika mused. "It's time to take a break."

"You could be right. I refuse to be with someone who's *constantly* flirting with other men."

"You shouldn't put yourself through that, Nigel. You're too good for him."

"I did love him once," Nigel sighed, in an over dramatic fashion. "Now the bloom has faded."

"It happens."

"I suppose so."

"Touch told me Kareema was the hit of the party," Shemika said, attempting to get him off the subject of Marcello. She wanted to hear more about Kareema, painful as it was.

"Ah, yes," Nigel enthused. "Exquisitely beautiful and such a style!"

"Seems everyone loved her."

"What's not to love? She's divine. As for Touch's brother, *oh, my God*! Quite the hunk. Did you speak to him?"

"Never got a chance," she answered, her heart beating fast. "Uh…did you?"

"I *wish*!"

"What time is Kareema coming in today?" she asked,

quickly changing the subject again because she didn't want to think about Famous. Not at all.

"Sometime this morning. Apparently, she and Alexia are old friends."

"That's convenient."

"Isn't it, though?"

"Well, I guess I'd better go call my mother back and try to do some work."

"Stay calm now," Nigel warned. "No fighting. You know how Carolyn *loves* to press your buttons."

"I promise."

She left Nigel and shut herself in her office where she sat for a while doing nothing. The nice thing about arriving at work early was the lack of activity. No noise and people rushing around. No ringing phones and nonstop action.

Just peace and calm.

She turned on her computer and stared at a bunch of e-mails she didn't feel like answering. She had no intention of calling her mother back. Carolyn would be full of complaints about her so-called rudeness in running out on her own rehearsal dinner, and she wasn't in the mood to listen.

Later, she'd visit Megan again, and this time maybe Tyrese wouldn't be around.

Not being able to talk about the Famous situation was killing her. She needed advice desperately, and Megan was the only person she could truly trust.

***

As they strode down Park Avenue on their way to Red's house, Famous asked Krush what he thought of Kareema.

"She's a real charmer," Krush replied. "I'm surprised you're not more into her."

"Yeah," Famous agreed. "But here's the thing, Kareema is

the kind of girl you're crazy about for a while, then one day you wake up and go, 'hold on a minute. This woman is driving me freaking *nuts*.' Plus she's a sex maniac," he added, groping for a cigarette.

"And that's a bad thing?" Krush asked, laughing. "By the way, have I mentioned that you smoke too much?"

"Gimme a break," Famous groaned, "it's the only vice I've got left."

"Poor you."

"You know," Famous said casually, "I was thinking that Kareema should be in movies. If she came out to L.A., maybe you could introduce her to some producers. You've got connections, right?"

"C'mon," Krush said. "Everyone and their mother wants to get into movies. Not to mention every model who ever walked the runway. Now you want me to hook your girl-friend up?"

"She's *not* my girlfriend," Famous said, exhaling a stream of smoke. "She's got, whaddya call it? Star quality, that kinda deal. She's different."

"They're *all* different one way or another."

"What do you think? Should I persuade her to buy aone-way ticket to Hollywood?"

"Are you trying to get rid of her?" Krushasked, amused.

Famous grinned. "That's *exactly* my plan."

***

After asking Detective Rodriguez if he should call his lawyer, Touch decided it would be prudent to do so because he certainly needed someone there with him. The reality of what had taken place was only just beginning to sink in.

Sadiya was dead. Murdered. The mother of his child had been the victim of unspeakable and heinous violence. He shuddered to think what would happen once the press got their feral little teeth into the story. This tragedy would change everything.

Christ! It was only the beginning of the nightmare.

***

Lady J Bentley prepared for battle. She awoke early on Monday morning and dressed accordingly. Chanel, it was definitely a day for Chanel.

Red Bentley had failed to put in an appearance all weekend. She was not worried. If anything was certain in life it was that he was holed up in his "secret" apartment, surrounded by whores.

She decided that *she* would meet with his three sons, it was about time someone enlightened them on the ways of their father. Why shouldn't it be her?

Obviously Red was not showing up, so this was the perfect opportunity to have her say. And she would.

Oh, yes, there was no doubt about *that*.

Chapter Nineteen

Clad in a form-fitting white suit and a blouse with a plunging neckline, her long, flame-colored hair swept up, Isha did not look like a highly priced call-girl–more like an expensive trophy wife. Inka, a raven-haired beauty with plumped-up lips and slanted eyes, wore a similar suit in dark green, tightly belted.

Both women, already tall, wore four-inch sling-back heels, and carried large expensive handbags stuffed with sex-toys and cash.

When it came to his sexual pleasure, Red Bentley was an extremely generous man, and these two women had spent most of the weekend with him. It had cost him plenty, but he wasn't complaining. Quite the opposite. Sex for sale. It sure beats living with a woman he'd grown to hate. Lady J Bentley could go to hell for all he cared.

On Monday morning Red was still active. Earlier, he'd had both women going down on him simultaneously. The pleasure he'd experienced was intense, and best of all, neither of them talked. All he had to do was throw money at them, and they did whatever he required, no questions asked.

Now they were dressed and ready to spend the day with him, for a price. Two tall, striking beauties with the devil in their eyes and full, succulent lips.

Wait until Lady J Bentley got a look at what *he* was bringing home. If these two didn't send her packing, nothing would.

***

On her way to the library, Lady J passed Diahann, the housekeeper, she loathed.

"Excuse me, Lady Bentley," Fatima said, straining to be polite because the loathing went both ways. "I'm worried about Mr. Bentley. Would you happen to know where he is?"

Lady J gave her an imperious look. "Worried, are you?" she said icily. "And why would that be?"

"As I'm sure you're aware, Mr. Bentley has not been home all weekend," Fatima said. "You must be worried too."

"Certainly not," Lady J snapped. "I know exactly where he is. He's at his apartment, the one where he spends all his time fucking whores."

A startled Fatima took a step backwards. "*What* did you say?"

"You heard me," Lady J said, a spiteful gleam in her eyes. "Fucking whores. That's what your lord and master does when he's not here. *That*'s what turns him on. Now, get out of my way." She brushed past Fatima and swept into the library.

***

"God, I hate this house," Krush muttered as they stood outside.

"Me too," Famous said. "No fond memories here."

"I gotta feeling this is the last time I'm coming here," Krush mused.

"Yeah, I'm making myself that promise."

Famous rubbed his hands together. "You think Touch is inside?"

"Dunno. He might have a hangover. He seemed to have been enjoying himself last night, he certainly liked Kareema."

"Maybe we could arrange a switch," Famous suggested drily. "I'll take Shemika, he can have Kareema."

"That's more like it," Krush said, changing his cell to vibrate. "Baby bro's got a sense of humor."

"I'm trying," Famous said with a rueful grin, doing the same to his phone. "It's not easy."

"Okay, let's do this," Krush said, taking a deep breathand pushing the buzzer. "Let the final circus begin."

***

With his lawyer on the way over and Detective Rodriguez still bombarding him with questions, Touch called Krush at his hotel. This was a family crisis, and heneeded his brother by his side.

There was no answer from Krush's room at the Four Seasons, so he tried his cell. Voicemail instructed him to leave a message. "It's Touch," he said tersely. "Call me immediately when you get this. It's urgent."

People were now roaming all over Sadiya's apartment, a police photographer, forensics, another detective, this time a female, and several more cops who were busy dusting for fingerprints.

"How long do I have to stay?" Touch asked.

Detective Rodriguez threw him a canny look. "Nobody's keeping you here, Mr. Bentley," he said mildly. "You're free to leave whenever you like. You told me where you were last night, we'll check it out, and that'll be that."

"Jesus *Christ*!" Touch exploded. "You're making it sound as if I'm a suspect."

"Do you feel like a suspect?" Detective Rodriguezasked, lowering his glasses, and peering at him.

"No, I don't," Touch snapped. "In case you're forgetting, I just lost my wife."

"*Ex*-wife, Mr. Bentley," Detective Rodriguez corrected.

"You're about to get married again, remember?"

"You're one smart son-of-a-bitch, aren't you?" Touch said, glaring at him.

"I try to be as smart as I can. That's a detective's job."

"Screw you," Touch said, losing it. "My lawyer is on his way over."

"Just exactly why do you think you *need* a lawyer, Mr. Bentley?" Detective Rodriguez asked, stroking his moustache.

"Because of you and your dumbass questions," Touch raged.

"I'm sorry if my questions are disturbing you. They're merely routine. I wouldn't be doing my job if I *didn't* ask them."

"I'm sure."

"What really surprises me is that you haven't told me that you're a friend of the mayor. Usually, it's the first thing youbig-shots do."

"Oh, I see," Touch said furiously. "Now I'm a big-shot. Is that why you're taking this attitude?"

"No attitude, Mr. Bentley. As I said before, this isroutine, all in a day's work."

Touch couldn't wait for his lawyer to get there so thathe could straighten things out and leave. His ex-wife had been murdered. She was lying on her bed stabbed to death, and this asshole was questioning *him.*

In his mind he knew who'd done it, but he wasn't about to reveal that information to the detective. It would be bad enough when the press got hold of the story. If they ever discovered his marriage to Sadiya wasn't legal, that she was a bigamist and Camryn was illegitimate, they'd crucify him.

He was not about to tell his lawyer about Kashif either.

He'd confide in Krush, see what he had to say. Krush

might be an entertainment lawyer, but he certainly had access to criminal lawyers who could advise him on what to do if he needed them.

Where the fuck was Krush anyway?

He'd completely forgotten that they were all supposed to be meeting at Red's house. Seeing his father was the last thing on his mind.

Two maids arrived at the apartment and scampered into the kitchen like frightened mice, whispering to each other.

Touch walked into the kitchen. "Make everyone coffee," he instructed them. Irena, Sadiya's personal maid, was slumped at the kitchen table, staring into space.

Touch was worried about Camryn, Detective Rodriguez claimed he needed to talk to her since she was the one who'd found the body. "She's five years old," Touch said. "Why do you have to talk to her?"

"I need to ask a couple of questions."

"Didn't you hear what I said? She's *five*. You've got no right to question my daughter."

"We'll see," Detective Rodriguez said. "There's a female detective who'll speak to her."

"I suppose you consider Camryn a suspect too," Touch said sarcastically.

"Anything is possible," Detective Rodriguez replied.

"You *son-of-a-bitch*," Touch said, almost losing it.

As the confrontation was about to become heated, Elliott Minor, Touch's lawyer, arrived. He was a portly man, balding and suntanned. "I'm so sorry, Touch," Elliott said, patting his client on the shoulder. "This is shocking, *shocking.* Was it a home invasion?"

"That's what Detective Rodriguez thinks it might be," Touch said. "But since he's questioned me into the ground—"

"You don't have to answer anything you don't want to," Elliott advised.

"I'm sure he knows that," Detective Rodriguez interrupted. "Although usually nobody minds answering questions when they have nothing to hide."

"Kindly refrain from using that tone with me," Elliott snapped. "You know perfectly well that my client is not required to answer *anything*." A long beat. "You're not arresting him, are you?"

"Why would you think that?" Touch said furiously.

"Of course not," Detective Rodriguez said, fiddling with his moustache.

One of the maids entered the room bearing a tray of coffee. She poured Touch a cup with a shaking hand.

He took a gulp and burned his tongue. "They want to talk to Camryn," he informed Elliott.

"Camryn?" Elliott questioned, raising his eyebrows. "Why?"

"Because she discovered the body."

***

The butler ushered Krush and Famous into Red's house, directing them into the library, where they were surprised to find Lady J Bentley sitting on the couch.

"Where's Red?" Krush asked, not prepared to put up with another runaround.

"I imagine he's on his way," she replied, sipping chamomile tea from a delicately patterned China cup. "Can I have the maid get you boys anything?"

"On his way?" Krush said, ignoring her offer of refreshments.

"Doesn't he live here?" Famous asked, wishing he could light up a cigarette, but knowing she'd object.

"Apparently not this weekend," she said, with an icy smile. "I fear your dear father is becoming senile."

"Why'sthat?" Krush asked.

"He has an apartment; a place he thinks I have no knowledge of." She took a long pause, then added, "Hekeeps his whores there."

"Whores?" Famous repeated, exchanging a quick look with Krush. "Did you say whores?"

"That's right. Your father might be old, but he's still a very sexually active man." A meaningful pause, then, "Fortunately, not with me."

"Excuse me," Krush said sharply. "Are you sure we should be having this conversation?"

"Why not?" Lady J replied, cool and vindictive. "I thought before your father got here, I might share a few things with you."

"What things?" Krush asked, sensing trouble ahead.

"Well, for one, your gambling debt."

"How the *fuck* do you know about that?"

"Didn't you ever wonder why Patrick Sumter is putting so much pressure on you to pay up?"

"You know Patrick?" Krush said, shocked andsurprised.

"I do not. Red does."

"Jesus!"

"Exactly *who* do you think has been insisting Patrick threaten you to make sure you pay? It's all about controland teaching you a lesson."

"You've gotta be fucking kidding," Krush exploded."Red is behind this?"

"Please control your language. I hate to be reminded of your father," Lady J said. "And you," she added, turning to Famous. "Red had his spies in Milan trying to dig up dirt on you. He was hoping you'd fall back into the drug lifestyle, and when you didn't, he hired people to try to lure you. However, you still wouldn't bite, which made him decide youweren't worth the trouble."

"Oh, *great!*" Famous said.

"Here's a copy of one of his emails," she said, handing Famous a sheet of paper.

He read it quickly.

The boy's a fuck-up. He'll crash and burn all by himself.
Stop wasting my time and money.

Silently he handed the email to Krush, who scanned itand shook his head in disbelief.

"Why are you telling us this shit?" Famous asked, remembering all the times he'd been offered drugs over the past few months, and wondering which of his so-called friends had been working for Red.

"Oh, dear me. You *do* take after him, don't you?" Lady J, sighed. "Both of you use foul language, exactly like your father."

"None of us takes after him," Krush said angrily. "I can assure you of that."

She glanced at her Bentley Cartier watch. "Will Touch be here?" she inquired. "I have something important to tell him too."

"Go ahead," Krush said coldly. "I'll pass on the information."

"Please do, for I'm sure Touch will be interested to know that the reason the banks withdrew from his multi-million-dollar building project in Lower Manhattan is because Red *insisted,* they did so. He used his own leverage with the banks to make certain they listened to him. Some people would call it blackmail."

"This is *crazy*," Famous said, running his hand through his hair.

"Is that why we're here?" Krush asked. "So that *he* can keep on flexing what he considers his control over us?"

"I have no idea why he wanted you here. I was merely the messenger," Lady J said, maintaining a cool attitude. "I can only presume he wishes to torture you further, of which I can assure you that he is quite capable."

"How come you're telling us this stuff?" Famous asked.

"I felt it was time you knew what an evil man your father is."

"Like we don't already know that," Famous scoffed. "You wanna see the scars on my butt? You wanna talk about a bully and an abuser? You wanna meet my *mom*, a screwed up, emotionally wrecked drunk because of him. Oh yeah, we know all about Red Bentley."

"This is bullshit," Krush said impatiently. "Is Red coming here this morning or not?"

"I really don't know."

"Then we're taking off."

"Wait," she said, her voice a sharp command. "Before you go, there's something else you should know, something that affects each and every one of us."

"Hey, why stop now?" Krush said. "You're on quite a roll."

"Then I suggest you prepare yourself," Lady J said. "For I do not believe you're going to like what you hear."

Von Diesel

Chapter Twenty

"Hey," Chanel said, over the phone.

"Hey," Velvet responded, delighted to get a call from her new friend.

"What happened last night?" Chanel asked curiously. "You turn the big man down?"

"I listened to you."

"Right on, sister! Mr. Stud came back into the party looking pissed. Tristin's not used to getting turned down."

"I *am* going to his office later to play him my demo."

"Then stay cool," Chanel warned. "Cause now he'll try harder. No way you can weaken."

"I don't intend to."

"That's my girl," Chanel said. "Here's the deal. I called my friend Kelz at the Madison Modeling Agency and told him all about you. He'll see you today, only you gotta be there by noon."

"You actually did it?" Velvet said excitedly.

"When I say I'm gonna do something, it's done."

"That's amazing, Chanel."

"Kelz will be straight with you. If he thinks you got no chance, he'll tell you."

"Wow, how can I thank you?"

"Wait 'til something happens before you start thanking me." A quick pause. "Oh, yeah, how's Malshonda doing today? That girl was feeling *no* pain last night."

"Want to hear the news of the morning?"

"Go ahead, hit me."

"Malshonda left. She's moving in with Slick Jimmy."

"You *gotta* be shitting me? After *one* night?"

"That's what I said. But there's no talking to Malshonda once she makes up her mind. Now I'm looking for a roommate."

"You shouldn't be in too much of a hurry, 'cause this'll end in tears. Jimmy's a POW."

"What's a POW?"

"Pig on wheels."

"Huh?"

"An asshole who bones anything that moves."

"Shouldn't I warn her?"

"Don't sweat it. That girl's gonna find out soon enough."

After getting the details of where to see Kelz, Velvet put down the phone. She was worried about Malshonda, but she was also excited for herself. So much was happening, it was as if the fall she'd taken had opened up a Pandora's box of new things. Finding out about her father, the video shoot, Tristin, Malshonda moving out, now *this*, an appointment at a modeling agency. Maybe she wouldn't have to go back to work at the coffee shop either, although there was no way she'd dump on Aaron and Peaches the way Malshonda had, she'd give them a couple of weeks' notice.

Preparing to go see the modeling agent was not so easy without Malshonda around to check with. Usually, they consulted on what to wear, depending on what they were doing and where they were going. She'd never been on her own–it was kind of liberating.

She rifled through her closet, hating everything. It wasn't as if she had money to burn on clothes, and she certainly didn't have anything fancy to wear. Fancy wasn't her style anyway, so she slid into a pair of skinny beige pants, boots, and a white Gap T-shirt. With her long dark hair, creamy milk chocolate skin and mesmerizing green eyes, she was a knock-out in whatever she wore.

***

The Madison Modeling Agency was located in a building off Lexington, and Velvet made it just in time for her appointment. The walls in the reception area were lined with framed magazine covers of different models.

As soon as she walked in, she felt insecure. The girls on the covers were all so slinky and glamorous, and what was she? Pretty? Yeah, she was pretty but, as far as she was concerned, nothing special.

Don't think that way, her inner voice warned her. *You are special, you can do whatever you set your mind on. Get some confidence, girl.*

She marched up to the reception desk. "I'm here to see, uh...Kelz."

The Asian receptionist, who was more interested in talking on the phone, gave her a cursory glance. "And you are?"

"Velvet. Chanel arranged the appointment."

"I'll let him know you're here," the receptionist said. "Take a seat."

Velvet sat down and picked up a fashion magazine with Tyra Banks on the cover. She stared at the exotic-looking model. Now *this* girl was special.

After ten minutes, the receptionist told her to go in.

Kelz was sitting behind a large, cluttered desk. He was a chain-smoking, middle-aged white man, with fleshy features, a brown comb-over hairstyle, and bushy eyebrows.

"Velvet," he said, a cigarette stuck to his lower lip. "Come in. Sit down. Chanel speaks well of you."

"I didn't have much time to get ready," she explained, feeling inadequate in her simple outfit.

"Get ready for what?" Kelz asked, shuffling a bunch of papers on his desk. "The perfect photographic model is a blank canvas. It's up to the photographer and client to create the look. Chanel's a good judge. She seems to think you've got it, whatever it might be."

"I'm flattered."

"Don't be. It's not personal," he said, taking a gulp of Diet Coke from a can balanced precariously on the arm of his chair. "Where's your book?"

"Book?" she asked blankly.

"Photographs, dear," he said, cigarette ash falling on his desk. "A portfolio of photographs."

"I don't have any," she explained. "You see, I wasn't really thinking of being a model, it was Chanel who suggested I come see you. Actually, I'm a singer."

"How tall are you?" he asked, not at all interested in her other career goals.

"Five-eight."

"Too short for runway work."

"Oh," she said, wondering if that meant this interview was over.

"Your measurements?"

"I, I have no idea," she said, feeling like an unprepared idiot.

"I see," he said, drumming his fingertips on his desk. "No book, no photographs, she doesn't know her measurements, she's not that tall, but you *have* got a face that cries out for attention, so I'm sending you on a couple of go-sees today."

"What's a go-see?"

"Exactly what it sounds like," he said, blowing a stream of smoke in her direction. "You go see a client or a photographer, and they make up their minds whether they want to use you."

"Right," she said.

"If things work out and we decide to take you on, photographs are essential. We'll put you together with a photographer who'll do your book for free in exchange for you boosting *his* book. That way everyone's happy. He gets to photograph a beautiful girl; you get the photographs you need."

She nodded. He'd called her beautiful, surely that was a good sign. Right?

"Okay, then," he said, all business. "First appointment at two o'clock, second one at three. Do not be late to either of them. Oh yes, and when you're through, don't call us, we'll call you."

***

After leaving Kelz's office, Velvet grabbed a tuna sandwich at a nearby deli, then jumped a bus to Tribeca where the studio was located.

By the time she found it she was late, and her next appointment was all the way uptown on Eighty-third Street. With the heavy traffic she'd be lucky if she made it by four, let alone three. After that she had the most important meeting of the day, taking her demo to play for Tristin, and there was no way she could be late for that.

The first go-see was a joke. There were at least twenty other girls sitting around in reception, all with portfolios and cute outfits, all looking their best.

It was obviously an audition, not a go-see.

Figuring it wasn't worth staying around and missing the second appointment, Velvet turned and left. She stepped into the service elevator with a tall, skinny guy wearing overalls and a trucker baseball cap. He was balancing a large pizza box in one hand.

"Want a piece?" he asked, flipping open the lid.

"Aren't you supposed to be delivering that?" she asked.

"Nope. I'm supposed to be *eating* it," he said, grinning.

"Feel free to help yourself."

"No thanks. I just had a sandwich."

"You here for the audition?" he asked, helping himself to a hefty slice of pizza.

"I was, but there's too many girls waiting."

"You came all this way and you're not gonna see anyone?" he said, between chews.

"I can't stay around; I've got to be somewhere else at three. Do you work here?"

"Guess you could say I help out."

"What's the audition for anyway?" she asked curiously.

"A swimsuit layout."

"Like a *Sports Illustrated* kind of thing?"

"More like a *Stuff* or *Touchim,*" he said, going for a second slice of pizza.

"You know those magazines?"

"I've seen them."

"You're probably not the right type," he said, a dribble of tomato sauce sliding down his chin.

"You have to be a *type* to be in those kinds of magazines?"

"You gotta be a little more plump and round figured."

"Oh, *thanks.*"

"You got a great look, though," he said encouragingly. "You could do commercials."

His compliment softened her up. "I saw my first modeling agent today," she said, dying to confide in someone. "He sent me on two go-sees. This is the first, but he didn't tell me anything about either of them."

"Gimme your name and agency, and I'll mention you were here and couldn't stay."

"Velvet. The Madison Modeling Agency. Won't they think it's rude that I left?"

"At least I can tell them you made the effort."

"Thanks, and enjoy your pizza," she said, as the creaky elevator ground to a halt.

"I will," he said, still busily chewing. "Good luck with theother job."

She made the second go-see with minutes to spare.

There were no other girls present, just a mannish-looking woman sitting alone in a photographer's loft.

The woman looked her over, asked a few questions,took a couple of Polaroids, then sent her on her way.

She left feeling dizzy and hopeful, thinking that maybe, just maybe, she was finally heading for the break she'd been wishing for all her life.

Von Diesel

Chapter Twenty-One

"Where we going?" Isha asked, sitting in the back of Red Bentley's Rolls-Royce, and admiring her reflection in a small gold compact. She'd stolen it from the dressing room of a woman whose husband had been using her services while his wife was out of town.

"I do not pay you to ask questions," Red growled. "Questions are not part of your job."

Isha ignored his rudeness. She didn't give a shit. As long as the money kept coming, who cared?

Inka adjusted her skirt so that the chauffeur, who could barely concentrate on his driving, got a clearer view of her snatch. Like Isha, Inka never wore underwear unless it was at a client's request.

Both women had seen *Basic Instinct* several times.

Both women fancied themselves in the Sharon Stone role. Tough, fearless, sexy, predatory, they were true admirers of American cinema.

Isha yawned. The decrepit old billionaire was a sex-mad little bugger. He'd wanted the entire sex menu, and then he'd wanted more. "What we do if he dies on us?" she'd asked Inka, who was more experienced when it came to dealing with very old, sex-crazed billionaires.

"Take all his cash and run like hell," Inka had joked.

"Here's what I require you girlies to do," Red said, breaking into Isha's thoughts. "When we get to my house, you walk in, one on each side of me. There'll be people there who'll probably insult you. Ignore 'em. Say nothing."

"People insulting me cost more," Isha stated, clicking her gold compact firmly shut.

"Me too," agreed Inka.

"How much more?"

"'Double our agreement.'"

Red cackled. He admired women who knew how to make a deal.

***

"Come in, dear," Alexia Ciccone said, gesturing for Shemika to enter her office. "Meet my friend and our new signature model, Kareema. Kareema, say *buongiorno* to one of my best PR girls, Shemika Scott-Simon."

"*Ciao!*" Kareema exclaimed, as if they were old friends. "It is *you*."

"You two know each other?" Alexia asked.

"Last night, I was at a party for Shemika and Touch Bentley," Kareema said, looking stylish and sexy in a Dolce & Gabbana charcoal, wool, pinstripe pantsuit. "My *ragazzo*, Famous, is Touch's younger *fratello*. Famous do the photographs with me. You'll fall in love with him, Alexia. *Every* woman falls in *amore* with my Famous. He's *delizioso, si?*" she said to Shemika, who stood transfixed to the spot.

Shemika nodded silently. So Famous was the male model in the photographs with Kareema. Famous was working for Ciccone. Could *anything* be worse?

"Where *was* this party?" Alexia asked, bristling because she hadn't been invited.

"It was my rehearsal dinner," Shemika quickly explained. "I didn't spend much time there because my friend, Megan, went into labor, and I left to go with her and her husband to the hospital."

"Touch is *molto bene*, you are *buena* girl." Kareema sighed. "He is *bello*, rich, and, how you say in your country? Sexy. Is he sexy?" she added in a teasing voice. "*Molto* sexy?"

"Excuse me?" Shemika said, taken aback.

Kareema gurgled with laughter, all gleaming white teeth and lightly tanned, glowing skin. "If he is anything like my Famous, you are one very *contento* woman."

"When do *I* get to meet Famous?" Alexia asked, holding out her hand and admiring her blood-red manicure.

"Today," Kareema said casually. "He be here later."

"Did you need me for something?" Shemika asked, realizing she'd have to come up with an excuse to leave work early if she didn't want to see him again, which, of course, she *did*.

"Ah, yes," Alexia said, tapping her tapered fingers together. "It would be excellent for Kareema and myself to have lunch with Liz Smith."

"Today?" Shemika questioned, startled. Did Alexia honestly believe that Liz Smith would be free on a moment's notice?

"If Liz can manage it," Alexia said airily. "If not, maybe tomorrow. What day you do photographs, Kareema?"

Kareema shrugged. "I'm not sure."

"Let me ask Nigel," Shemika said, desperate to get out of Alexia's office. "I'll call Liz and get back to you. I'm sure she'd love to meet Kareema."

"She *should*," Alexia said haughtily. "Kareema is the most famous model in Italy. During fashion week who does *every* designer bag for?" A dramatic pause. "Kareema and Naomi Campbell. No other model can touch them."

"I'm sure," Shemika muttered, dying to leave. "Is there anything else?" she asked, trying not to let her feelings show.

"No," Alexia said, dismissing her with an arrogant wave.

"Wait," Kareema said. "If this Liz, whoever she is, cannot lunch with us today, how about *you*, Shemika?"

"Oh, no," Shemika said quickly. "I usually grab something at my desk. I couldn't possibly encroach on your time with Alexia."

"Is okay," Alexia said, smiling at Shemika in a patronizing way. "Is not usual I lunch with my staff, but today I make exception. You come with us, Shemika."

"I'd love that," Shemika said, thinking, *I can't imagine anything I'd like less.* "Uh, let me go find out if Liz Smith is available and I'll get back to you."

She fled from Alexia's office. She'd been trying to put a good face on things, but seeing Kareema in the light of day, the reality of it all sunk in. She'd slept with this gorgeous supermodel's boyfriend, and even though he'd turned out to be Touch's brother, she couldn't stop thinking about him. Which was sick, *really* sick.

It was supposed to have been a fling, a tempestuous one-night fling to prepare her for a great marriage, a *safe* marriage, where she'd be with Touch forever, and they'd have fantastic sex and live happily ever after.

Only she and Touch hadn't had sex yet, and judging from last night, it wasn't going to be *that* fantastic.

Touch hadn't called today. Was he mad about last night? Did he think she'd come on too strong?

If he thought that she was too aggressive, it was ridiculous she was *marrying* the man. They had to work things out.

She decided to give him a buzz, then she thought, no, let him call her. *He* was the one who'd rushed her out of his apartment.

She hurried to find Nigel who was working in the design room. "When is Kareema doing the photographs?" she asked.

"The shoot is set for tomorrow," Nigel said, studying a series of sketches.

"And your favorite Italian also wants to know who the photographer is."

"Ah…the fantastic Antonio," Nigel replied, starry-eyedat the thought of being in the presence of such a famous photographer. "We should all be there, you, me, Sassy and Chinky. There'll be a catered lunch and scads of champagne. It will be an amazing day."

"Exactly what I need," Shemika said irritably.

"You sound a tad snippy."

"I am."

"Why?"

"Alexia wants me to have lunch with her and Kareema."

"I'd be *honored* if Alexia asked *me* to lunch," Nigel said, suffering a momentary twinge of jealousy. "And you're not pleased?"

"How can I sit there with those two women all through lunch? It's not my thing."

"M*ake* it your thing, dear," Nigel said sagely. "If youwant to move up in this company, *make* it your thing."

***

After fetching Nanny Reece and Camryn from a downstairs apartment, Elliott Minor allowed the female detective to question Camryn for five minutes. Touch didn'tlike it, but as Elliot explained to him, nobody had anything to hide and it was best to cooperate. *Nobody has anything to hide*, Touch thought grimly. *I do. I have Draygo Kashif to hide. And what am I going to do about that?*

It was a problem, because telling what he knew about Draygo Kashif would open up an investigation that might be disastrous for not only him but Camryn as well. He was more concerned about his little daughter than anything else. Thescandal and publicity would turn him into a joke, but for Camryn it would be even worse. She would be branded forever as the illegitimate child of the murdered Russian bigamist.

After speaking to the detective, a frightened and subdued Camryn ran straight into his arms. "I want my mommy," she whimpered, cuddling up to him. "Somebody hurt my mommy."

"It'll be alright, sweetie," he assured her, enveloping her in a hug. "Daddy is taking care of everything."

Nanny Reece was now in the other room talking to Detective Rodriguez. Touch needed to speak with Elliott, so he carried Camryn into the kitchen, switched the TV to a cartoon channel, instructed the maids to watch her for a few minutes, then went to find Elliott.

"What's going on?" he demanded. "I have to get Camryn and her nanny out of here."

"Be patient, Touch," Elliott counselled. "Let's not antagonize anyone."

"Don't talk to me about antagonizing people," he said angrily. "That detective has been nothing but rude to me."

"I understand, Touch. Calm down, I'll settle this."

"You don't *get* it, do you, Elliott?" he said through gritted teeth. "They're treating me as if I'm a suspect."

"It's routine to question the husband, especially the *ex*-husband."

"I'm not your average ex-husband," Touch said, steaming. "You think I look like some construction worker who stabs his wife to death in a drunken rage?"

"Stay calm, Touch."

"Quit telling me to stay calm," he snapped. "My daughter is in shock. Fucking Nanny is talking to a detective, and I WANT TO GET OUT OF HERE."

"I understand," Elliott said. "I'll see what I can do." He left the room and returned almost immediately. "I've just been advised that there is press downstairs."

"Are you kidding me?" Touch said, outraged. "How did the press find out?"

"They listen in on police scanners. They have spies in the police department. They find out everything."

"I am *not* talking to the press," Touch fumed.

"I know that. I'll arrange for your driver to meet us in the underground garage."

"This is a nightmare, Elliott."

"Life goes on," Elliott said, spewing out a suitable cliché. "You'll get over this."

"Easy for you to say," Touch said, storming back into the living room.

Five minutes later, Elliott came to find him. "Detective Rodriguez informed me that you're free to go."

"He said that, did he? So, he can run and check out my alibi. Christ! I need to talk to my brother." As soon as he mentioned Krush, he remembered the early-morning meeting with Red he'd failed to attend. "That's why I can't get hold of him," he muttered.

"Who can't you get hold of?" Elliott inquired. "My brother, Krush."

"I'm glad you have family to turn to, this is a sad day. Sadiya was a lovely woman."

"No, she wasn't," Touch contradicted, shaking his head. "Sadiya was a money-hungry social-climber. *You* know that better than anyone. *You* were the one who went through my divorce with me."

"I'm sure she didn't deserve to die like this," Elliott said, uncomfortable with Touch's harsh words.

"You're right," Touch replied, suddenly weary. "Nobody deserves that."

Von Diesel

Chapter Twenty-Two

Before Lady J Bentley was able to reveal anything more to Krush and Famous, Red Bentley made his entry into the library, flanked on either side by Isha and Inka.

They made a bizarre trio. The old billionaire and the two high class call-girls, both towering over him in their tight-fitting suits and stiletto heels.

"Sorry I'm late," Red said, not sorry at all. "I'm sure Janey here has been keeping you entertained."

Lady J remained seated on the couch, her eyes shooting daggers. "Red," she said, in a deceptively quiet tone. "We're *so* glad you could make it. I was filling the boys in on a few things I thought they should know." Her eyes swiveled to take in Isha and Inka. "Do introduce us to your friends."

She managed to make "friends" sound like the dirtiest word in the dictionary.

"Can't remember their names." Red cackled. "Only the size of their tits."

Meanwhile Isha had spotted Krush and he'd recognized her. Brazenly, she flaunted his stolen watch on her wrist, daring him to say anything.

He didn't. He was smart enough to stay silent and watch this scenario play out.

Inka was busy checking out Famous. She had a weakness for hot young guys. She winked at him, a wink that promised, *For you, I'm available and free.*

"It looks like you're busy," Krush said, not wishing to become involved in the scene that he knew was about to take place, "so I guess this meeting which, by the way, never happened, is over."

"Over?" Red roared. "It hasn't even begun."

"Too bad," Krush responded. "Because I never did like the

circus, even when I was a kid."

"You always were the one with the mouth," Red said, bobbing his head up and down. "Shame you're so weak. You could've made something of yourself if you weren't such a loser."

"Yeah," Krush said, remaining surprisingly calm. "I could've been like you, right? A miserable old bastard hanging out with hookers thirty years younger."

"Let's go, Krush," Famous said, realizing just how nasty this could get if they didn't make a fast exit.

"Oh," Red said, turning to glare at his youngest son. "The fuck-up has a voice."

"*You're* the fuck-up," Famous retaliated, immediately losing it. "You and your billions think you control everything. Well, here's a news flash. You can't control us."

"I can't, huh?" Red shouted. "Is that why you all came running to New York when I summoned you? Run, run, run. Pick up your ticket and run to daddy. What did you think? That I was on my death bed? That you were about to inherit my money? Is that why you came?"

"I came because I thought you might've changed," Famous muttered. "Crazy, huh? To think I had a father who might've cared."

"Red will never change," Lady J said, still maintaining her composure. "I think we all know that."

"You're still here," Red said, feigning surprise. "Thought I told you to pack up and get out."

"Apparently, I didn't hear you," she said. "Perhaps I was too busy reading your will, which I was on the point of telling your sons about. I'm sure they'll be as fascinated as I was."

"You know *nothing* about my will," Red snarled. "We'll see about that."

Isha was getting bored. Family dramas were not her thing, she'd had enough of her own back in Slovakia. Idly, she wondered about the woman sitting on the couch. An angry, repressed woman wearing Chanel and a very tasty diamond watch. Was she the old man's wife? Mistress? Whoever she was, she was one furious bitch and quite frankly, Isha couldn't blame her. What woman wouldn't be angry if their husband or lover walked in with two incredibly sexy women on each arm?

"Excuse me, Mr. Bentley." Fatima had entered the room. With all the shouting going on, nobody had heard her knock.

Isha and Inka both turned to inspect the newcomer. She was black and quite attractive in an understated way. Late thirties, dressed in drab clothes, she could be a knock-out if she tried.

"*What?*" Red yelled, not pleased with the interruption.

"It's the phone for Krush," Fatima said, giving Isha and Inka a disapproving look. "It's Touch, he says it's very important."

"I'll take it," Krush said, glad for the diversion. Fatima handed him the phone and he walked over to the other side of the room. "Where are you?" he asked, in a low voice. "You won't believe what's going on here."

"Meet me at my apartment," Touch said urgently. "Something terrible has happened. Sadiya's dead. She's been murdered."

* * *

Naturally, Liz Smith could not make lunch given such short notice, so Shemika was stuck. She rode in the car with Alexia and Kareema to the Grill Room at the Four Seasons restaurant. The two Italian women jabbered away in their native tongue, while Shemika sat next to Alexia's driver feeling like a hostage on her way to anexecution.

She'd already decided there was nothing to dislike about Kareema. The Italian supermodel was unbearably beautiful and just as charming as everyone said. The more time Shemika spent with her, the more she was unable to understand why Famous had cheated on such a gorgeous woman. Grandma Poppy was right. All men were dogs. All men cheated. Except Touch. She was sure he wouldn't cheat because he had too much character, which was why she loved him.

Yes, I do love him. Come on.

Lunch at the Grill Room was a ritual. The spacious restaurant was crowded with various power players who occupied their usual tables. See and be seen.

Kareema was certainly seen, heads turned as the stunning supermodel followed Alexia to their table.

Shemika trailed behind the two flamboyant women, feeling totally miserable. She wondered what time Famous was showing up at the House of Ciccone. If they ran into each other, would he acknowledge her? Or was he prepared to ignore their one night of incredible, mind-blowing, fantastic sex? She wondered if he was thinking about her as much as she was thinking about him.

She *had* to get over to the hospital and discuss the situation with Megan. Somehow or other she was determined to make a daring escape from this abysmal lunch.

***

Pacing round his apartment waiting for Krush to get there, Touch knew he should call Shemika and tell her before she heard it on the news. Not only were the press downstairs in Sadiya's building, but they were also gathered outside his apartment building, both being part of the Touch Bentley's empire. This would make their story even juicier.

He'd already called David Santana and apprised him of the situation. "You'll have to deal with the Japanese," he'd said. "If they're not happy with that, reschedule my meeting with them for the morning."

David had assured him he'd do everything he could to persuade them to come up with the money.

Touch was hoping that when he contacted Shemika, she would offer to collect Camryn and take her away from the explosion of publicity he knew was about to happen. Sadiya Bentley was hardly a nobody, she'd been married to *him*. The woman had courted publicity; she'd made sure she was part of the New York social scene. This was a headline story.

"I want my mommy," Camryn cried, coming into his bedroom, tears streaking her pretty little face. "When can I see my mommy?"

"Soon, baby," he said, trying to sound cheerful. "How about you watch a DVD of *Finding Nemo* or *The Incredibles* with Nanny? Is that a plan?"

"No *Finding Nemo*! No *Incredibles*!" Camryn shouted, stamping her foot. "I WANT MY MOMMY!"

"Christ! Where was Nanny Reece when he needed her?" He found her in the kitchen on the phone. "Who are you talking to?" he demanded, paranoid that she might be working out a deal with the *National Enquirer* to sell her story.

"I'm sorry, Mr. Bentley," Nanny Reece said, all crisp and English. "I'm booking a ticket home to England. America is not for me. I cannot take the violence."

"You can't do that," he said, quite staggered that she would even contemplate deserting Camryn at a time like this.

"Oh, I think I can," she said, tight-lipped.

"You'd leave Camryn?"

"I'm sorry, Mr. Bentley, I have to go."

"What if I double the salary you're getting now?"

"It's not a question of money."

Damn the woman! She wasn't any good anyway, she paid absolutely no attention to Camryn. He should have noticed it before, and Sadiya *certainly* should've noticed.

"When are you leaving?" he asked, resigning himself to the situation.

"This afternoon."

What an inconsiderate incompetent *cow*. If this was her attitude, they were better off without her.

***

"We have to go," Krush said to Famous, clicking off the phone. "Touch has an emergency."

"Why isn't Touch here?" Red demanded. "More financial disasters he's not man enough to handle?"

"You'd enjoy that, wouldn't you?" Lady J said, joining in. "Perhaps you can find *another* bank to blackmail, forcing them to withdraw from Touch's big building project."

"How dare you speak about matters that don't concern you?" Red said, his face darkening with anger.

"I can speak about anything I want," she responded, her composure intact.

Krush was already at the door. "Put on the TV," he suggested. "Find out for yourselves what's going on."

Red was furious, he had not had the opportunity to make his planned announcement to his sons. It was all Jane's fault, she'd ruined everything. "You see these lovely young ladies?" he said, giving her a spiteful glare. "They'll be moving in here with me."

Isha and Inka exchanged a startled look that was news to

them.

"How *nice* that you plan to fill your house with whores," Lady J said, remaining icy and controlled. "According to the private papers I read, along with your Will, you always *did* enjoy helping out whores. So, I suggest that if you do not wish me to make my information public, you will work out a very generous settlement with my lawyer. Only *then* will I leave this house."

She arose from the couch, and without so much as glancing at Isha and Inka, swept out of the room.

"Moving in?" Isha said. "Not me."

"What do you mean, not you?" Red growled. "For enough money you'll get down on all fours and lick my boots if I order you to."

"What do you think it will cost you for us to move in?" Inka questioned, always the businesswoman. "Possibly more money than you're even prepared to spend. We are *very* expensive girls."

"How do *you* know what I'm prepared to spend?" he said, narrowing his eyes.

"Your wife seems serious about getting a big settlement," Isha remarked. "The bitch means business."

"She's *not* my wife," he said, scowling.

"She sure acts like one," Isha said, smoothing down the jacket of her tightly fitted suit.

"What's with her anyway?" Inka added. She certainly doesn't like you."

Red decided he didn't want to keep them around after all, they talked too much, they asked questions, they were getting on his nerves. It was one thing when they were striding around his apartment, naked, giving him intense pleasure. But somehow, in his house, they were just two over-made-up hookers. Besides, he had to clear things up with Jane. How *dare* she pretend she knew all his secrets? *Nobody* knew all of Red Bentley's secrets, that was for sure.

"The two of you can get out now," he said, still scowling.

"We're happy to leave," Inka responded, "as soon as you've paid us."

"I've paid you plenty. Now go."

"Not enough for *this* trip." Isha snorted derisively.

"Jesus Christ!" he said angrily. "You're nothing but two greedy whores."

"And that's just the way you like us, isn't it?" Inka said.

"Yes," Isha agreed, fingering her stolen Rolex. "Especially when your little cock is in our tight mouths, andyou're coming all over our tits."

"Get out!" he shouted, reaching into his pocket, and tossing a handful of hundred-dollar bills at them.

"You know where to find us when you need our services again," Inka said pleasantly, always thinking ahead.

"GET OUT OF MY HOUSE!" Red screamed.

The two women picked up their money and made their exit, leaving the room filled with the aroma of their expensive perfumes. Muttering to himself, Red clicked on the TV.

"What's going on?" Famous asked, following Krush out to the street.

"You won't believe this," Krush said, flagging down a cab.

"Fill me in, then I'll tell you whether I believe you or not."

"It's Sadiya."

"Touch's ex?"

"That's right. According to Touch, she's been killed."

"Huh?"

"Murdered was the word he used. *Murdered.*"

***

After pushing a salad around her plate while Kareema and Alexia continued to chat animatedly in Italian, Shemika finally spoke up, claiming she wasn't feeling well.

"I come with you to the ladies' room," Kareema announced, full of concern. "You sit for a minute, we put wet cloth on your forehead. You feel better."

"No, no, really, it's just a splitting headache," Shemika said, determined not to get caught in any more traps. "Ms. Ciccone," she added, appealing to Alexia, 'do you mind if I leave?'

Alexia shrugged. She couldn't have cared less. "Take Alexia's car back to your apartment," Kareema offered. "You call later to say how you feel."

"*Scuse?*" Alexia said, irritated that Kareema felt free to offer her car to one of her minions. "Get a cab, Shemika. Put it on your expense account."

"Thanks," Shemika said, jumping up.

Once out of the restaurant she walked a couple of blocks, waved down a cab and told the driver to take her to the hospital, where she hoped to find Tyrese gone.

Maybe, if she was lucky, she'd finally get to speak to Megan.

***

Several TV trucks, crews and on-air talent were out on the street, with a scattering of photographers, taking up key positions outside Touch's apartment building

"Keep your head down and walk right in," Krush warned. "They don't know us. And if they ask any questions, we know nothing."

"Got it," Famous replied.

Krush paid the cab, and they made a dash inside.

The officious desk clerk stopped them. "Who're youhere to see?" he demanded.

"Touch Bentley," Krush said. "Tell him his brothers are downstairs."

The desk clerk called up to Touch's apartment, then motioned them to the elevator. "The penthouse," he said.

"What else do you think Lady J was about to tell us?" Famous asked as they entered the elevator.

"Who knows? She's got something on her mind, and it's obviously something he'd prefer we didn't hear from her."

"How about him walking in with those two hookers from Touch's bachelor party?" Famous said, lighting up a cigarette and inhaling deeply. "*That* was a scene and a half."

"You wanna hear the kicker?" Krush said. "One of them was the girl who stole my watch."

"The *your-cock-needs-a-service girl?*"

"Right on."

"Shit!"

Touch was waiting at the door of the elevator. Hehugged them both. "Thanks for coming," he said, looking wrecked. "It means a lot."

"Just take it easy," Krush said, putting his arm round his older brother's shoulders, "and tell us what happened."

"Let's go in the living room," Touch said wearily. "I think I could manage a drink."

By the time Shemika got back to the hospital, Megan's room was overflowing with flower arrangements, celebratory balloons, and baby gifts. To Shemika's relief, Tyrese was nowhere in sight.

Megan's face lit up when she saw Shemika. "I'm desperately trying to feed the little tyke," she wailed, holding baby Tyrese close to her breast. "Believe me, it'snot as simple as they tell you."

"It doesn't *look* simple," Shemika remarked, checking out the cards on the flower arrangements. Naturally there was a tasteful vase of mixed roses from Nancy–a woman who prided herself on always being socially correct.

"I'm glad you're back," Megan said enthusiastically. "I need to hear *everything*."

"It's like I told you earlier," Shemika said, perching on the end of the bed. "It turns out Mystery Man is Touch's *brother*."

"That's so *not* good news."

"Exactly," Shemika said grimly. "Now tell me, what am I supposed to do about *that?*"

"There's nothing you *can* do."

"That's helpful, Megan," she said. "I mean, should I make out like we've never met before, that we haven't been in bed together and shared fantastic sex? Am I supposed to pretend it never happened?"

"Maybe a conversation would be in order," Megan suggested. "Only if he didn't say anything to you. Why would *you* be the one to open it up?"

"Because I *have* to," Shemika insisted.

"When are you doing this?" Megan asked.

"I don't know," she wailed, as her cellphone buzzed. "Oh God, I'm so confused," she added, checking out caller ID. "It's my mother," she said, grimacing. "I'm not taking it."

"Why?"

"You *know* why. She'll be full of complaints about me leaving last night."

"I'm sure she's not mad," Megan said, gesturing to an overcrowded side table. "Look at the beautiful roses she sent me."

"Ha! That's *her* doing the right thing. If I know my mother, she's mad all right."

Almost immediately the phone next to Megan's bed started ringing. Megan reached over and picked up. "Hi, Tyrese," she said, snuggling the baby even closer. "Tyrese Junior is doing well. I've got a feeling he misses you. He's so *cute,* his eyelashes are getting longer, along with every-thing else." She paused to listen for a moment. "Shemika," she said urgently. "Put on the TV. Go to CNN."

"Why?"

"Just *do* it."

And there it was, all over the news, the story covering Sadiya's murder.

Chapter Twenty-Three

Tristin held her face and kissed her with an intensity she'd never experienced before. Some men could kiss, and some men couldn't. Tristin was a master.

Velvet closed her eyes, allowing herself to be swept up in the moment.

How was this happening? How had this adventure begun? And where would it end? Tristin was married, taken, unavailable.

And yet...she couldn't stop herself getting lost in his arms. His lips were driving her crazy, his tongue exploring her mouth, his hands starting an exploration of their own.

It took all of her willpower, but somehow or other, she managed to push him away.

"What?" he said impatiently.

"You're married," she stated.

"You got something against marriage?"

"No."

"Hey, I could tell you my wife doesn't understand me," he said, smiling lazily. "The deal is she understands me big-time. We, uh, kinda got an arrangement."

"It's not my—"

Before she could finish what she was about to say, he was kissing her again and his hands slowly working their way under her sweater.

Oh, God! Why was this happening? Arrangement or not, he belonged to another woman, and she wasn't prepared to share.

She'd arrived at his office promptly at six-thirty, although she almost hadn't made it. After the second go-see, she'd raced home and changed clothes. She'd put on a soft white sweater, chocolate brown cargo pants, and brown furry boots, purposely not wearing anything provocative. She'd gone for serious as opposed to sexy, tying her long dark hair back in a ponytail and adding some tinted winter shades she'd picked up for ten bucks from a shopping cart. They were a copy of a Chanel pair, and they looked cool, although she realized they'd last about ten minutes before they snapped in two.

"Hello there, LL," he'd said, greeting her with a brief hug. "Looking good."

"Hi," she'd responded, breathing in his expensive after-shave, her eyes darting around his office checking out the gold records and plaques on the walls, the award statues including several Grammys and many other awards. On his huge Perspex desk stood a silver-framed photo of his wife, the Princess Toshi.

"Sit," he'd said, indicating a comfortable leather couch.

Damn! She was intimidated by all the trappings of his success. He was Tristin Juzang, and who was she? Just another would-be singer scratching for a break.

"Gimme," he'd said, reaching out for her demo iPhone.

She'd handed it over, knowing he'd hate it, shivering with the anticipation of defeat.

There were two songs on her Soundcloud , both her own compositions. They were edgy, with lyrics true to her heart, but they certainly weren't hip-hop or rap.

He'd put on her music and sat back behind his desk lis-tening intently, his face expressionless, leaving her no clue as to what he was thinking.

She'd sat on the couch across from him, fists clenched, sweat trickling down her back, totally freaked out with nerves.

When the two songs were finished, he'd stood up, walked over to her, and somehow or other the kissing had begun.

She knew she should've shoved him away immediately, not allowed anything to get started. But she was so damned anxious to know what he had to say about her music. It was the reason she was here. The reason she existed.

And he'd said nothing.

Now he was kissing her, groping her. It was a cruel and unusual punishment, yet she didn't want him to stop.

Finally, she summoned the strength to push him away again. "My music," she began, trying not to sound too needy. "That's why I'm here."

"Is *that* why you're here?" he asked, smoky eyes all over her.

"You *know* it's why I'm here," she said, swallowing hard.

"Nothing else?" he questioned, giving her that look of his. That sexy, knowing look.

"Like what?" she said, pretending she didn't know what he was talking about, although the sexual tension was steaming up the room.

"Hey, surely you understand that you and me, we got something special going on," he said, those eyes of his working their usual magic.

Desperately, she tried to conjure up Chanel's words of warning, *He's 'bout as married as a dude can get...No different from all the other horndogs out there...Tristin's always out to score the prize...He's never gonna change...*

"Look," she said, making a supreme effort not to weaken, "special or not, you're *married,* so this has to be strictly business. Either you're into my music or you're not."

"And how about if I was into it, you think that'd score mepoints?"

"Points?"

"A little sugar and cream?"

"No," she said, refusing to meet his eyes, they were too damn tempting.

"Man, you're cold," he complained. "Cold and hot at the same time. Irresistible combination, baby, and you know it."

"I guess you're not interested in my music," she said, sucking up her disappointment that he was–after all–just another horny guy with one thing on his mind.

"Hey, don't get all uptight on me–you *do* have some-thin'. I dig your voice. It's Mary J. Blige mixed with a little bit of Alicia Keys. Husky. Sexy. You got soul, girl. I like that."

"Really?"

"You *know* you're cool. Gotta get that confident vibe goin'. Course, it's not the kinda stuff I usually put out on my label, but I'm thinking I'll get you together with a producer who'll know what to do with you."

"You'd do that?" she asked hopefully, not sure whether to believe him or not.

"Gotta do something to keep you coming back," he said, throwing her one of his killer smiles. "Right, babe?"

And it was then that she realized Malshonda was right–she'd fallen in love with a married man. And how dumb was that?

Before things progressed further, she decided she'd bet-ter get the hell out of there. It was too dangerous to stay. She was too attracted to him–and, as she kept on reminding herself over and over, HE WAS MARRIED! Plus, mixing business with pleasure was never cool.

"I have to go," she said, edging towards the door.

"Yeah?" he said, following her. "What's the panic?"

"I'm working," she lied–the same lie she'd used on Kev.
"Blow it off."

"I can't."

"Thought we might grab a bite," he said, moving evencloser.

"Just you, me and your wife?"

"What is it with you?" he said, giving her a quizzicallook. "All this wife shit is getting old."

"Uh…did I mention that I have a boyfriend?" she said,backing away from him.

"Is that supposed to scare me off?" he said teasingly, his eyes all over her.

"No," she said breathlessly. "Your *wife* is supposed to scare you off."

"Oh, man!" he said,laughing.

"What?" she said, thrown by his cavalier attitude. "Seems you're more concerned about my wife than I am."

"Because I'm the one who'll get hammered if she findsout you're playing on her."

"My wife wouldn't mess with you," he assured her.

"Why not?" she asked boldly.

"Because I wouldn't let her."

"Word is she's a wild thing when it comes to watching out for you."

"No, baby, *you*'re the wild thing," he said, taking another step towards her. "I can feel it on your lips. It's in those crazy green eyes of yours, that body…"

"I have to go," she said quickly, her hand on the door. He handed her a black card engraved with gold lettering. "In case you get home and change your mind,here's my *private* cell number. You never know, LL, you could get *real* hungry later…"

"When can I meet with the producer?" she asked, thinking that if she stuck to business somehow, she'd be safe.

"Tomorrow," he said, watching her intently. "Same time, same place."

"I'll be here." And before he could get any closer, she was out of there, almost running into the elevator while trying not to think about how irresistibly attractive she found him.

Tristin Juzang. Who would've thought a few days ago he'd be coming onto her this way? She'd served him coffee for weeks on end and he'd ignored her, acted as if she didn't exist. Now *this*. He'd even given her his private number.

It was crazy, yet exhilarating. *And* he was putting her together with a producer in spite of the fact that she wasn't falling into his bed or his car or the couch in his office.

Wow, he's something else, she thought. *I could really go for him.*

But it's not going to happen, her stern inner voice warned. *Because falling in lust with Tristin Juzang would be the worst damn thing you could do.*

Back at the apartment, the answering-machine she shared with Malshonda was flashing five messages. They were probably all for Malshonda. They usually were.

She opened a can of Campbell's tomato soup and poured it into a pan to heat it. It occurred to her that if she wasn't so full of principles, she could be sitting in a fancy restaurant eating lobster and steak with Tristin. Then later she could be falling into his bed, making wild passionate love.

But hey, she *did* have principles and nothing was going to happen sexually, just career-wise. That was all she asked for. Let him help her get some kind of singing career started.

For a moment she thought about the way he'd kissed her.

It was so damn hot. Tristin Juzang was some fucking great kisser. The best.

The *married* best. Married, married, *married.* Had to keep reminding herself.

The soup was bubbling, so she grabbed a bowl, poured it in, and sat at the counter that separated the minuscule kitchen area from the living space.

While she was eating, she leaned over and pressed the button on the answering-machine.

Message one: *Malshonda, it's Moose, and it's Monday. You was supposed to phone me, woman, and I'm waiting. Don't be keeping me waiting like this.*

Message two: *Hey, babe, Kev here, but you know that. Just got called on another outta town gig. I'm leaving tonight, so later.*

Message three: *Velvet, it's Mom. Please call me back, it's important.*

Message four: *Hi, Velvet, Kelz here. Congratulations. You got the job. Contact the agency immediately when you receive this message.*

She leaped up, pressed repeat, and listened to Kelz all over again. *You got the job!* How fantastic was *that*? Oh, man, the woman who took the Polaroids must've liked her. Unfortunately, she had no clue what the job was.

She wished Malshonda was around to share her good news, but no, Malshonda had moved out.

Grinning to herself, she played message five, it was Fatima again. What did *she* want?

Before she could find out, Kelz called a second time. "Aren't *you* the lucky girl?" he said. "Three days in Malibu. They want you on a ten o'clock plane to L.A. tonight."

"Excuse me?" she said, stunned.

"Look, I'm at the theatre with my wife, so I can't talk. I

hope you're about to say yes, Velvet, because I can assure you that opportunities like this do not happen everyday."

"Tonight?" she said, her head spinning. "I have to leave tonight?"

"That's what I said. Thirty thousand, all expenses paid. The agency takes a thirty-five per cent commission. Are you on e-mail?"

"Uh...no," she mumbled, thinking, *Did he just say thirtythousand?*

"Then I'll fax you papers to sign."

"I–I don't have a fax machine," she stuttered, still inshock.

"They've booked you into *Shutters* in Santa Monica, I can fax you there. There'll be a car to pick you up at LAX. And an e-ticket waiting for you at the United desk at Kennedy. This is your shot, Velvet. Do *not* blow it. *Bon voyage.*"

Chapter Twenty-Four

Touch's main concern was getting Camryn settled somewhere safe, far away from the prying eyes of the press. Fortunately, Shemika came through. As soon as she heard the news she rushed over to his apartment, full of concern and care. "Oh, Touch," she said, hugging him tightly. "I'm so sorry. It's such a terrible tragedy."

"I know," he responded, holding onto her.

"Did they break in? Was it a robbery?" she asked, extracting herself.

"That's what the detectives seem to think."

"I don't know what to say. It's just awful, Touch. I wish there was something I could do."

"There is. I'd like you to take Camryn for a couple of days. Her nanny's quitting on me, and Camryn shouldn't be around here with the press setting up camp outside."

"There's no question, I'll take her. It's the very least I can do."

"Thanks, sweetheart, it means a lot to me."

"Don't *wanna* go, Daddy," Camryn muttered, lower lip quivering when he informed her that she was going home with Shemika. "Wanna stay here with you."

"You can't, sweetie," he explained. "Daddy's got things he has to take care of, important things."

"Then I want my mommy," Camryn said, putting on a stubborn face. "Where's my mommy?"

"We had to take Mommy to the hospital, but she's going to be okay, and she wants you to spend the night with Shemika."

"We go see Mommy, Daddy," Camryn said hopefully. "Just you and me. We go see her *now*!"

"Soon," he promised.

"Then Camryn stay here with Nanny."

"Nanny Reece has to fly back to England."

Camryn's pretty face crumpled. "Why, Daddy? *Why*?"

"Because she does. Don't worry, sweetie, Shemika will take care of you. It's only for a day or so."

"Do I have to go with stupid Shemika, Daddy?" Camryn said, scowling.

"Please don't call Shemika names," Touch warned. "It's not nice."

Famous stepped forward and scooped Camryn up into his arms. "Hey, pretty girl, how about I go too? Is that okay with you?"

"Yes!" Camryn squealed, her scowl turning into a coquettish little smile. "My uncle come too."

"Thanks," Touch said gratefully, as Camryn snuggled up to Famous. "That'd be a big help."

Shemika was silent. She was horrified enough about Sadiya's brutal murder, and now she was going to have to deal with Famous. This wasn't the right time for them to sort out what had happened between them.

"I'll call you later," Touch said, kissing Shemika's cheek as he accompanied the three of them to the elevator. "Take care of my girls," he said to Famous. "They're both very precious."

"Yeah," Famous said. "I'll do my best."

As the elevator doors closed, Shemika turned to Camryn. "We're going to have so much fun," she said brightly.

"No, we're not," Camryn responded. "We're not! We're not! We're *not*!" Shemika exchanged a quick look with Famous.

"It'll be fine," he mouthed.

Easy for *him* to say. He wasn't a quivering, nervous, guilt-ridden wreck.

***

After everyone left, Touch began filling Krush in on the Kashif story, including Sadiya's threat to have the man taken care of.

Krush listened intently. "And you think he took care of her instead?" he said thoughtfully when Touch was finished.

"That's exactly what I think," Touch replied, his expression grim.

"But you can't be sure?"

"I'm sure alright. Kashif is an evil son-of-a-bitch with a big agenda. He was after money and plenty of it. Somehow Sadiya must've got in his way, so he decided to get rid of her."

"Shouldn't you tell the detectives what you know?"

"Are you *shitting* me?" Touch exploded. "Have you any idea what the press would do to me if they got hold of the truth? They'd crucify me. And what do you think they'd do to Camryn? She's *illegitimate,* Krush. And God knows what Sadiya did back in Russia, it's possible she was a prostitute."

"Then you're not telling the detectives anything?" Krush said, frowning. "You're allowing this Kashif to walk around loose, a suspected murderer?"

"I need to see if Sadiya kept any documents concerning him."

"What about close girlfriends? Someone she might've confided in?"

"I doubt it. All Sadiya cared about was running with the social set. She was relentless–only interested in who had the most money and what charity board she should get on that would elevate her social position."

"You didn't know she was like that when you married

her?"

"Unfortunately, not."

"Too bad," Krush said. "You could've saved yourself a lot of grief."

"Do you think I don't know it?"

"Well, if you want my advice, you should tell the detectives everything. Let them get into it, that's their job."

"I appreciate your concern, but I have to wait."

"For *what*?"

"Kashif."

"It's your call."

"I know," Touch said, walking over to the window. "Have you *seen* what's going on downstairs?" he muttered, peering out. "The press are getting ready for a siege. You do realize that the entire family will be involved. Red, you, possibly even Shemika. And—"

"Not me," Krush interrupted quickly. "I'm not part of this family."

"You're my brother," Touch stated grimly. "They'll find a way to drag you into it."

"I've never traded on the Bentley name," Krush pointed out.

"You think I have?"

"None of us did, so there's no reason why we'd get brought into it."

"The media will start digging for anything they can."

"I'm a lawyer," Krush said, scratching his chin. "They say or print anything inaccurate, and I'll sue their asses."

"Keep that thought. It's not going to stop them."

"You don't think so, huh?"

"Not the *New York Press*. They're relentless."

"You missed the morning meeting with Red,"

Krushsaid.

"Is he leaving us everything?" Touch asked sarcastically.

"He walked in with two hookers on his arm."

"Am I supposed to be surprised?"

"Lady J was sitting in the library pissed as a cat on a hot tin roof as he marched in, bold as shit."

"Friday, he fails to turn up, and today you're telling me he walks in with hookers. What kind of game is he playing?"

"Who knows?"

"I'd better call David Santana," Touch said, glancing at his watch. "He was meeting with the Japanese bankers onmy behalf."

"Before you make the call," Krush said, "you should know that Lady J let it drop it was Red who forced the U.S. banks to withdraw from your building project. Seems he has that kind of leverage."

"What?" Touch said, shocked and angry. "Red is responsible?"

"She showed us copies of his e-mails to the banks involved."

"That conniving bastard!"

"Sorry, Touch, he really screwed you."

"So, you realize what that son-of-a-bitch has put me through? I could lose everything."

"Guess what? Me too. Remember my gambling debt? Well, the pressure to pay is apparently coming from Red. It wouldn't surprise me if he's a major shareholder in the fucking casino. He's got his bony fingers in every pie."

"Jesus Christ!" Touch said, still steaming. "Nothing changes, does it?"

"Hey, the bastard can't beat us with a stick, so he devises other ways to punish us. Dear old Dad, always full of any crap he can hand out."

***

Standing in the elevator as it descended to the lobby, Famous glanced over at Shemika. She was staring straight ahead, her perfect face quite impassive. "You okay?" he asked, in a low voice, wondering what she was thinking.

"Thank you, yes," she replied, trying not to look at him. She was not okay at all. Her stomach was churning, and she felt sick.

"Uh...I guess we need to talk," he said tentatively.

"Not now," she said, staring pointedly at Camryn. The little girl was busily sucking her thumb, her arms firmly clutched around Famous's neck.

"I didn't mean now," he said, remembering the incredible softness of her skin and the way she smelled of soap and perfume and all things nice.

"Maybe later," she said hesitantly, for she knew they couldn't continue to ignore what had happened between them. She didn't know about him, but for her the tension was a killer.

"Definitely later," he agreed, thinking how vulnerableand pretty she looked in spite of everything.

Touch's car was waiting downstairs in the garage. The three of them got in and the driver whisked them straight to Shemika's apartment.

As soon as they walked into her place, she felt awkward. Having Famous on her territory was extremely uncomfortable, they'd shared such intimacy, yet they were still virtual strangers.

"Uh...can I get you anything?" she asked, glad that she'd tidied up before leaving in the morning. Unlike her mother, who had maids on twenty-four-hour call, she preferred to have a cleaning lady come in only once a week, something Carolyn never stopped complaining about.

"No, thanks," he said, removing Camryn's arms fromaround his neck and putting the little girl down.

"Wanna see a movie," Camryn said, immediately aware that she was not the center of attention.

"I'm afraid I haven't got any children's DVDs,"Shemika said helplessly.

"Anything in particular you'd like to see, pretty girl?"Famous asked, bending down to her.

"Wanna see *The Incredibles*," Camryn said, in a high-pitched voice. "Wanna see it with you."

"Maybe we should take her out for something to eat," Shemika suggested. "I've got nothing here. There's a coffee shopon the corner."

"You hungry, Cam?" Famous asked.

"Wanna see *The Incredibles*," Camryn repeated.

"Okay, here's the deal," he said. "You, me and Shemika will go downstairs to the video store and buy you the DVD of *The Incredibles*, then we'll take you for a burger. You like big fat burgers with onions and relish and all the trimmings?"

"Mommy says I mustn't eat hamburgers," Camryn said primly.

"Special treat," he said. "Burgers and French fries, and after that we'll come back here and watch the movie. How does *that* sound?"

"Only if you carry me," Camryn said, quick as a flash. "Carry me! Carry me! *Carry me!*"

"I can't carry you everywhere we go," he said, laughing. "You're too heavy. You're like a big lumpy sack of potatoes."

"Potatoes," Camryn repeated, almost cracking a smile.

"Big sack of lumpy potatoes*!*"

"That's right, little girl."

"I'm *not* little."

"Fine–*big* girl. How's that?"

"Carry me! Carry me! *Carry me!*" Camryn chanted.

"Okay, okay," he said, sweeping her up into his arms again. Then, glancing at Shemika, he said, "You know,Kareema and I, we're not a couple."

"You don't have to explain anything to me," she said, thinking how patient and understanding he was dealing with his niece.

"I thought you should know. That's all."

"Now I do." *And it makes no difference. I'm engaged toTouch, and that's that.*

"Okay, Cam," Famous said. "We're going on an adventure. Let's blow this pop stand."

"Pop stand!" Camryn said, bursting into a fit of giggles."Pop stand! Pop stand! Pop stand!"

****

Isha was looking forward to getting back to her apartment. Weekend jobs were not her favorite, even though they paid handsomely. She'd worked long and hard to have her own apartment, and now that she did, she enjoyed her time alone.

One of her rules was never to entertain any of her clients at home. It was either their place, a suitable venue, or a hotel. She made no exceptions.

Walking in, she was dismayed to find her cousin Igor sprawled on her pristine white couch in front of her new flatscreen TV, stuffing potato chips into his mouth.

"What the hell you doing here?" she demanded. "I told you not to use my key. You're supposed to phone first."

Igor gave her an unconcerned look. "I'm your cousin," he said reproachfully. "Do not speak to me like that. What's itmatter to you anyway?"

"You were away all weekend; didn't think you'd mind."

"You *know* I mind," she said bad-temperedly. "I like myprivacy."

"Privacy," he scoffed. "How much *privacy* do the johns you spend all your time with give you?"

"My *clients* pay lot of money," she said, stepping out of her shoes. "And *you* never object to taking some of it."

Igor was her favorite cousin, the only family member who'd made it to America. She had a soft spot for him, but he was always getting himself caught in "situations", and she was always helping him out.

Sometimes she wished he'd find himself a legitimate job and stop sponging off her.

"I'm in a...situation," he said. "It's best I no go back to my place for a day or so."

"Why?" she said accusingly. "What you done now?"

"Nothing," he answered, yawning. "Just bringing you gift because you nice cousin."

"What gift?" she asked suspiciously.

"Good one," he said, scratching his belly."Let me see."

Raising his body from the couch, he fumbled in his jacket pocket and produced a string of perfect white pearls.

Isha grabbed them, held them up to the light andinspected them with a practiced eye. "Is real?" she asked, although as a canny connoisseur of jewelry she was quite sure that she already knew the correct answer.

"Of course, it's real," Igor replied indignantly. "Very excellent quality. Cost me a lot."

"Liar," Isha said, fixing the pearls around her neck, noticing the intricate diamond clasp shaped like a flower, and wondering where he'd come across such a prize. She was no longer mad. Real pearls were real pearls, and they went nicely with her recently acquired Rolex.

All in all, it had been quite a profitable weekend.

To Be Continued…
The Billionaire Bentleys 3
Coming Soon

The Billionaire Bentleys

Lock Down Publications and Ca$h Presents assisted
publishing packages.

BASIC PACKAGE $499
Editing
Cover Design
Formatting

UPGRADED PACKAGE $800
Typing
Editing
Cover Design
Formatting

ADVANCE PACKAGE $1,200
Typing
Editing
Cover Design
Formatting
Copyright registration
Proofreading
Upload book to Amazon

LDP SUPREME PACKAGE $1,500
Typing
Editing
Cover Design
Formatting
Copyright registration
Proofreading
Set up Amazon account
Upload book to Amazon
Advertise on LDP Amazon and Facebook page

***Other services available upon request. Additional

Von Diesel

charges may apply
Lock Down Publications
P.O. Box 944
Stockbridge, GA 30281-9998
Phone # 470 303-9761

Submission Guideline

Submit the first three chapters of your completed manuscript to ldpsubmissions@gmail.com, subject line: Your book's title. The manuscript must be in a .doc file and sent as an attachment. Document should be in Times New Roman, double spaced and in size 12 font. Also, provide your synopsis and full contact information. If sending multiple submissions, they must each be in a separate email.

Have a story but no way to send it electronically? You can still submit to LDP/Ca$h Presents. Send in the first three chapters, written or typed, of your completed manuscript to:

LDP: Submissions Dept
Po Box 944
Stockbridge, Ga 30281

DO NOT send original manuscript. Must be a duplicate.

Provide your synopsis and a cover letter containing your full contact information.

Thanks for considering LDP and Ca$h Presents.

Von Diesel

NEW RELEASES

JACK BOYS VS DOPE BOYS by ROMELL TUKES
KILLA KOUNTY 2 by KHUFU
IN A HUSTLER I TRUST by MONET DRAGUN
THE COCAINE PRINCESS by KING RIO
TOE TAGZ 4 by AH'MILLION
A GANGSTA'S QUR'AN by ROMELL TUKES
THE BILLIONAIRE BENTLEYS 2 by VON DIESEL

The Billionaire Bentleys

Von Diesel

3X KRAZY III

STRAIGHT BEAST MODE II

De'Kari

KINGPIN KILLAZ IV

STREET KINGS III

PAID IN BLOOD III

CARTEL KILLAZ IV

DOPE GODS III

Hood Rich

SINS OF A HUSTLA II

ASAD

RICH $AVAGE II

MONEY IN THE GRAVE II

By Martell Troublesome Bolden

YAYO V

Bred In The Game 2

S. Allen

CREAM III

By Yolanda Moore

SON OF A DOPE FIEND III

HEAVEN GOT A GHETTO II

By Renta

LOYALTY AIN'T PROMISED III

By Keith Williams

I'M NOTHING WITHOUT HIS LOVE II

SINS OF A THUG II

TO THE THUG I LOVED BEFORE II

The Billionaire Bentleys

IN A HUSTLER I TRUST II

By Monet Dragun

QUIET MONEY IV

EXTENDED CLIP III

THUG LIFE IV

By **Trai'Quan**

THE STREETS MADE ME IV

By **Larry D. Wright**

IF YOU CROSS ME ONCE II

By **Anthony Fields**

THE STREETS WILL NEVER CLOSE II

By K'ajji

HARD AND RUTHLESS III

THE BILLIONAIRE BENTLEYS III

Von Diesel

KILLA KOUNTY III

By Khufu

MONEY GAME III

By Smoove Dolla

JACK BOYS VS DOPE BOYS II

A GANGSTA'S QUR'AN V

By Romell Tukes

MURDA WAS THE CASE II

Elijah R. Freeman

THE STREETS NEVER LET GO II

By Robert Baptiste

AN UNFORESEEN LOVE III

Von Diesel

By **Meesha**

KING OF THE TRENCHES III
by **GHOST & TRANAY ADAMS**

MONEY MAFIA II

LOYAL TO THE SOIL II

By **Jibril Williams**

QUEEN OF THE ZOO II

By **Black Migo**

THE BRICK MAN IV

THE COCAINE PRINCESS II

By **King Rio**

VICIOUS LOYALTY II

By **Kingpen**

A GANGSTA'S PAIN II

By **J-Blunt**

CONFESSIONS OF A JACKBOY III

By **Nicholas Lock**

GRIMEY WAYS II

By **Ray Vinci**

KING KILLA II

By **Vincent "Vitto" Holloway**

Available Now

RESTRAINING ORDER **I & II**

By **CA$H & Coffee**

LOVE KNOWS NO BOUNDARIES **I II & III**

By **Coffee**

RAISED AS A GOON I, II, III & IV

BRED BY THE SLUMS I, II, III

BLAST FOR ME I & II

ROTTEN TO THE CORE I II III

A BRONX TALE I, II, III

DUFFLE BAG CARTEL I II III IV V VI

HEARTLESS GOON I II III IV V

A SAVAGE DOPEBOY I II

DRUG LORDS I II III

CUTTHROAT MAFIA I II

KING OF THE TRENCHES

By **Ghost**

LAY IT DOWN **I & II**

LAST OF A DYING BREED I II

BLOOD STAINS OF A SHOTTA I & II III

By **Jamaica**

LOYAL TO THE GAME I II III

LIFE OF SIN I, II III

By **TJ & Jelissa**

BLOODY COMMAS I & II

Von Diesel

SKI MASK CARTEL I II & III

KING OF NEW YORK I II,III IV V

RISE TO POWER I II III

COKE KINGS I II III IV V

BORN HEARTLESS I II III IV

KING OF THE TRAP I II

By **T.J. Edwards**

IF LOVING HIM IS WRONG…I & II

LOVE ME EVEN WHEN IT HURTS I II III

By **Jelissa**

WHEN THE STREETS CLAP BACK I & II III

THE HEART OF A SAVAGE I II III

MONEY MAFIA

LOYAL TO THE SOIL

By **Jibril Williams**

A DISTINGUISHED THUG STOLE MY HEART I II & III

LOVE SHOULDN'T HURT I II III IV

RENEGADE BOYS I II III IV

PAID IN KARMA I II III

SAVAGE STORMS I II

AN UNFORESEEN LOVE I II

By **Meesha**

A GANGSTER'S CODE I &, II III

A GANGSTER'S SYN I II III

THE SAVAGE LIFE I II III

CHAINED TO THE STREETS I II III

BLOOD ON THE MONEY I II III

The Billionaire Bentleys

A GANGSTA'S PAIN

By J-Blunt

PUSH IT TO THE LIMIT

By **Bre' Hayes**

BLOOD OF A BOSS **I, II, III, IV, V**

SHADOWS OF THE GAME

TRAP BASTARD

By **Askari**

THE STREETS BLEED MURDER **I, II & III**

THE HEART OF A GANGSTA I II& III

By **Jerry Jackson**

CUM FOR ME I II III IV V VI VII VIII

An **LDP Erotica Collaboration**

BRIDE OF A HUSTLA **I II & II**

THE FETTI GIRLS **I, II& III**

CORRUPTED BY A GANGSTA I, II III, IV

BLINDED BY HIS LOVE

THE PRICE YOU PAY FOR LOVE I, II ,III

DOPE GIRL MAGIC I II III

By **Destiny Skai**

WHEN A GOOD GIRL GOES BAD

By **Adrienne**

THE COST OF LOYALTY I II III

By Kweli

A GANGSTER'S REVENGE **I II III & IV**

THE BOSS MAN'S DAUGHTERS I II III IV V

A SAVAGE LOVE **I & II**

Von Diesel

BAE BELONGS TO ME I II
A HUSTLER'S DECEIT I, II, III
WHAT BAD BITCHES DO I, II, III
SOUL OF A MONSTER I II III
KILL ZONE
A DOPE BOY'S QUEEN I II III
By **Aryanna**
A KINGPIN'S AMBITON
A KINGPIN'S AMBITION **II**
I MURDER FOR THE DOUGH
By **Ambitious**
TRUE SAVAGE I II III IV V VI VII
DOPE BOY MAGIC I, II, III
MIDNIGHT CARTEL I II III
CITY OF KINGZ I II
NIGHTMARE ON SILENT AVE
THE PLUG OF LIL MEXICO II

By **Chris Green**
A DOPEBOY'S PRAYER
By **Eddie "Wolf" Lee**
THE KING CARTEL **I, II & III**
By **Frank Gresham**
THESE NIGGAS AIN'T LOYAL **I, II & III**
By **Nikki Tee**
GANGSTA SHYT **I II &III**
By **CATO**

The Billionaire Bentleys

THE ULTIMATE BETRAYAL

By **Phoenix**

BOSS'N UP **I , II & III**

By **Royal Nicole**

I LOVE YOU TO DEATH

By **Destiny J**

I RIDE FOR MY HITTA

I STILL RIDE FOR MY HITTA

By **Misty Holt**

LOVE & CHASIN' PAPER

By **Qay Crockett**

TO DIE IN VAIN

SINS OF A HUSTLA

By **ASAD**

BROOKLYN HUSTLAZ

By **Boogsy Morina**

BROOKLYN ON LOCK I & II

By **Sonovia**

GANGSTA CITY

By **Teddy Duke**

A DRUG KING AND HIS DIAMOND I & II III

A DOPEMAN'S RICHES

HER MAN, MINE'S TOO I, II

CASH MONEY HO'S

THE WIFEY I USED TO BE I II

By Nicole Goosby

TRAPHOUSE KING **I II & III**

Von Diesel

KINGPIN KILLAZ I II III

STREET KINGS I II

PAID IN BLOOD **I II**

CARTEL KILLAZ I II III

DOPE GODS I II

By **Hood Rich**

LIPSTICK KILLAH **I, II, III**

CRIME OF PASSION I II & III

FRIEND OR FOE I II III

By **Mimi**

STEADY MOBBN' **I, II, III**

THE STREETS STAINED MY SOUL I II III

By **Marcellus Allen**

WHO SHOT YA **I, II, III**

SON OF A DOPE FIEND I II

HEAVEN GOT A GHETTO

Renta

GORILLAZ IN THE BAY **I II III IV**

TEARS OF A GANGSTA I II

3X KRAZY I II

STRAIGHT BEAST MODE

DE'KARI

TRIGGADALE I II III

MURDAROBER WAS THE CASE

Elijah R. Freeman

GOD BLESS THE TRAPPERS I, II, III

THESE SCANDALOUS STREETS I, II, III

The Billionaire Bentleys

FEAR MY GANGSTA I, II, III IV, V

THESE STREETS DON'T LOVE NOBODY I, II

BURY ME A G I, II, III, IV, V

A GANGSTA'S EMPIRE I, II, III, IV

THE DOPEMAN'S BODYGAURD I II

THE REALEST KILLAZ I II III

THE LAST OF THE OGS I II III

Tranay Adams

THE STREETS ARE CALLING

Duquie Wilson

MARRIED TO A BOSS I II III

By Destiny Skai & Chris Green

KINGZ OF THE GAME I II III IV V VI

Playa Ray

SLAUGHTER GANG I II III

RUTHLESS HEART I II III

By Willie Slaughter

FUK SHYT

By Blakk Diamond

DON'T F#CK WITH MY HEART I II

By Linnea

ADDICTED TO THE DRAMA I II III

IN THE ARM OF HIS BOSS II

By Jamila

YAYO I II III IV

A SHOOTER'S AMBITION I II

BRED IN THE GAME

Von Diesel

By S. Allen
TRAP GOD I II III
RICH $AVAGE
MONEY IN THE GRAVE I II

By Martell Troublesome Bolden
FOREVER GANGSTA
GLOCKS ON SATIN SHEETS I II

By Adrian Dulan
TOE TAGZ I II III IV
LEVELS TO THIS SHYT I II

By Ah'Million
KINGPIN DREAMS I II III

By Paper Boi Rari
CONFESSIONS OF A GANGSTA I II III IV
CONFESSIONS OF A JACKBOY I II

By Nicholas Lock
I'M NOTHING WITHOUT HIS LOVE
SINS OF A THUG
TO THE THUG I LOVED BEFORE
A GANGSTA SAVED XMAS
IN A HUSTLER I TRUST

By Monet Dragun
CAUGHT UP IN THE LIFE I II III
THE STREETS NEVER LET GO

By Robert Baptiste
NEW TO THE GAME I II III
MONEY, MURDER & MEMORIES I II III

The Billionaire Bentleys

Von Diesel

THE STREETS WILL NEVER CLOSE

By K'ajji

CREAM I II

By Yolanda Moore

NIGHTMARES OF A HUSTLA I II III

By King Dream

CONCRETE KILLA I II

VICIOUS LOYALTY

By Kingpen

HARD AND RUTHLESS I II

MOB TOWN 251

THE BILLIONAIRE BENTLEYS I II

By Von Diesel

GHOST MOB

Stilloan Robinson

MOB TIES I II III IV V

By SayNoMore

BODYMORE MURDERLAND I II III

By Delmont Player

FOR THE LOVE OF A BOSS

By C. D. Blue

MOBBED UP I II III IV

THE BRICK MAN I II III

THE COCAINE PRINCESS

By King Rio

KILLA KOUNTY I II

By Khufu

The Billionaire Bentleys

MONEY GAME I II
By Smoove Dolla
A GANGSTA'S KARMA I II
By FLAME
KING OF THE TRENCHES I II
by **GHOST & TRANAY ADAMS**
QUEEN OF THE ZOO
By **Black Migo**
GRIMEY WAYS
By Ray Vinci
XMAS WITH AN ATL SHOOTER
By Ca$h & Destiny Skai
KING KILLA
By Vincent "Vitto" Holloway

BOOKS BY LDP'S CEO, CA$H

TRUST IN NO MAN

TRUST IN NO MAN 2

TRUST IN NO MAN 3

BONDED BY BLOOD

SHORTY GOT A THUG

THUGS CRY

THUGS CRY 2

THUGS CRY 3

TRUST NO BITCH

TRUST NO BITCH 2

TRUST NO BITCH 3

TIL MY CASKET DROPS

RESTRAINING ORDER

RESTRAINING ORDER 2

IN LOVE WITH A CONVICT

LIFE OF A HOOD STAR

XMAS WITH AN ATL SHOOTER

The Billionaire Bentleys

CPSIA information can be obtained
at www.ICGtesting.com
Printed in the USA
LVHW010246020422
714934LV00010B/1143